The Spiral Garden

The Spiral Garden

Louise Cooper

The BRITISH FANTASY SOCIETY

First published in Great Britain in 2000 by

The British Fantasy Society
201 Reddish Road, South Reddish,
Stockport, SK5 7HR

The Spiral Garden
Copyright © 1989, 1995, 1997, 2000 Louise Cooper

'Cry' First appeared in *Other Edens III*,
Edited by Christopher Evans & Robert Holdstock, Unwin, (1989)

'The Spiral Garden'
First appeared in *Realms Of Fantasy* (August 1997)

'His True and Only Wife'
First appeared in *Realms of Fantasy* (April 1995)

'Birthday Battle'
First appeared in *The Mammoth Book of Fairy Tales*
Edited by Mike Ashley, Robinson, (1997)

'St Gumper's Feast' (Previously unpublished)

Introduction copyright © 2000 Diana Wynne Jones
Illustrations copyright © 2000 Clive Sandall
Photograph copyright © 2000 Clive Sandall

Edited for the British Fantasy Society by Jan Edwards

The right of Louise Cooper to be identified as the Author of the Work has been asserted by her in accordance with the Copyright, Designs and Patents act 1988. All rights reserved. No part of this publication may be reproduced, stored in a retrieval system or transmitted in any form or by any means without the prior written permission of the author, nor be otherwise circulated in any form of binding or cover other than that in which it is published and without a similar condition being imposed on the subsequent purchaser.

ISBN 0-9524153-7-2
(paperback) BFS 007
British Library Cataloguing in Publication Data.
A catalogue record for this book is available at the British Library.

Contents

Introduction by Diana Wynne Jones	9
Cry	13
The Spiral Garden	29
His True and Only Wife	49
The Birthday Battle	77
St Gumper's Feast	91
Bibliography	116

This book is respectfully dedicated to Giant Bolster, mythical hero of St Agnes in Cornwall, whose personal badge appears on the front cover. And to John, Ian, Bob, Soozie, Bill, Mark, Helen, Jane, Guy, Derek and all the other lovely people who make up his crew when he comes out to celebrate the summer.

Introduction by
Diana Wynne Jones

Louise Cooper is one of the writers photographed by Patti Perrett in her Hugo-nominated *Faces of Fantasy*. Patti is a highly specialised genius. She caught every one of her subjects posed so characteristically and in surroundings so apt that you know at a glance what each person is *like* and can also get a fair idea of the way they write. She photographed Louise like this (and, yes, she did me too, as Greer Gilman put it 'queening it in a carven chair'!) in a way that says a whole lot about Louise.

Louise is photographed seemingly at the borders of a strange landscape, standing just inside it, so that she could almost be a design for a Tarot card. It is not clear if this landscape is wild or tame, except that the dark truncated cones of the trees in it seem to have been clipped to that shape. There is a suggestion of mystery in the distance. Louise herself, in a stance that is both regal and diffident, seems to be saying, 'This is my kingdom. Would you like to come and look?'

When I asked Louise about this picture, it turned out to be indeed her kingdom — or one of them. She explained that it was the garden of an old monastery that had been destroyed in the Reformation. Just beyond the photographed portion there is a stone arch full of statues in niches and each statue has had its head lopped off when the monastery was destroyed. These truncated statues and the queer trees, she explained with the diffidence that comes out in the photo, actually gave her the idea for the story called *The Spiral Garden:* combine the trees and the statues and give the result a twist. And here you have the way in which a born writer creates a dark and moving story out of a static landscape.

There is no doubt that Louise is a born writer. She has all the hallmarks (including being born on the 29th of May, which I believe is the cusp of Spring and Summer in the old calendar: this was in Hertfordshire in 1952). One of the signs is that you start early and don't stop. By the time Louise was ten, she was writing so well that her stories were being read out to the class in her primary school. When, however, she won a scholarship in 1965 to St Albans High School for Girls, things did not go so well. She was writing ghost and horror stories still, but she developed a passionate hatred for school which does not surprise me: I just can't imagine Louise in a girls' High School - and for maths in particular - which *does* surprise me, because Louise is a dedicated and versatile musician and this usually goes with a strong bent for maths: I think it must have been very badly taught - and she left at the age of fifteen. Pursued by dire predictions from the headmistress. It must give Louise great pleasure now to have confounded those predictions.

By this time, she was writing full-length books. This is another mark of the writer-born. You have to tell a story and you have to tell it in full. Louise confesses that she prefers writing at novel length and does not feel wholly at ease with short stories, though, as you can see from this collection, she does them very well. But she is at her most confident spreading her narrative over one, three, or nine books. This is very characteristic of her. She has at least one world and several kingdoms in her head and needs to explore them, and then invite the rest of us to come and look.

But it could not have been easy, when she needed this kind of spaciousness in writing, having to support herself with various jobs. Louise at one time worked in publishing as a secretary and as a blurb-writer, but she also wrote romances under pseudonyms to earn money. Nothing seems to have stopped her writing. She was twenty-one when her first (official) book was published. This was *The Book of Paradox,* a quirky book, vibrant with talent, based around the Tarot - her early interest in the Tarot is something that comes out subliminally in Patti's photograph. This book was followed by *Lord of No Time* which, when it was later re-written and expanded into *The Time Master* trilogy, enabled Louise finally to support herself by her writing. That trilogy in turn expanded backwards and forwards into two more, showing that Louise had the space she needed at last.

In between, however, there were two horror books. The story *Cry* in this collection, remarkable for its sensory images, shows you what she can do with this genre. Then, as if that were not enough, Louise wrote - and continues to write - books for children. *Crown of Horn* and *The Blacksmith* are both based around another of her abiding interests, folklore and myth. She has an inwardness with these, and together with her feeling for the natural year and its cycles, they make a framework for all her writing. Sometimes this figures quite simply, as in the story *The Birthday Battle* in this collection, but more often myth and seasonal folklore make a rhythm in the background that holds her narratives in place.

And sometimes she does something else entirely, like her recent *Creatures* books for children, full of the near-to-home horror and yik that children love. One way and another, Louise has been averaging at least two books a year. You feel that where other people go to the Bahamas, Louise has a holiday by writing a different sort of book. She probably has more imagination than any other writer. She says, again with this endearing modesty of hers, that she is quite unable to imagine being without imagination, and adds that she thinks it might be a flaw in her, because she can't portray a character who has no imagination. This made me laugh rather. It seemed to me she had done just that with the complacent young man Carolan in her story *His True and Only Wife*. A few deft touches of smugness, and she makes you know exactly how it feels to be Carolan.

Louise has recently married the artist (and illustrator of these stories) Cas Sandall and moved to Cornwall. I was astonished, knowing both Louise and her writing, to find she had only just moved there. I had always assumed, so strongly that I never thought to ask, that Louise had lived in Cornwall all her life. She seems to belong there. Here her husband, being still new to the business of living with a born writer, is constantly amazed at finding Louise standing in their garden with a half-depotted plant in one hand and an earthy trowel in the other, lost to the world because she has had an idea and is in a book in a country somewhere else in the universe. You might say that Louise has entered one of her kingdoms. They describe this state as 'a kind of fugal daydreaming'. It overrides normal life and makes the basis for the regality that Patti picked up on in her photograph.

For there is never any diffidence about Louise's writing. It is strong and assured. The first thing I am struck by is always how emphatically visualised all her landscapes are. The story is always in a definite place and you can *see* that place - often a strange place and with extreme weather, but it is *there* as you react. Yet when you look, the impressive thing is how little actual description there is. Louise has visualised her kingdom so precisely that she only needs a few touches to make the reader see it too.

Against these landscapes and in these sharply seen places, her narratives unfold with the unexpected inevitability that you find in folk tales, ballads or Greek drama. It isn't that you know what is going to happen: it is more that when it does, you realise that it had to be like that. And the characters these inevitable-uninevitable things happen to seem to carry a little more weight than normal people do. They are by no means archetypes, but there is something more behind them, as there is with images in the Tarot. I have no idea how this is done, but it seems to have something to do with Louise's being soaked in myth, folktales and folk songs, and possibly with her wide knowledge of history too. As I said, these things form a pattern that contains the story.

Louise, however, says firmly that she never regards a particular pattern as inevitable. It is more that she makes a pattern of choices for her characters, which leads on in the wave of chaos theory. You can start with a butterfly's wing fluttering in a certain way, but this can take you onwards to something far-reaching and catastrophic.

Louise believes in justice, she says, and ethical justice at that, where the people who make the bad choices get what they deserve. But she also believes in karma. This is a sterner form of justice, where a certain choice brings a certain consequence, now or hereafter, whatever you happen to deserve. I think what makes most of her narratives so fascinating is the way these two kinds of justice are so often counterpointed in them. You can see this happening in *The Spiral Garden* and in *His True and Only Wife* on a small scale. It takes in whole kingdoms in her longer books.

I hope she goes on writing such things for at least another five decades.

CRY

No.
Yes.
No... Please... I can't. Please...
Don't plead. You must. You will. When the time comes. You'll know when that is.

And there was the dream, of blurred, pale faces framed against paler walls, and the heat of an unexpected Indian summer, close and humid and draining all the life from the air. And walls that pulsed in and out, in and out, like a heart struggling to beat against intolerable pressure. Voices murmuring concernedly, the clink of something small and metallic rattling against porcelain. One face among the blurs looked familiar, but a name wouldn't come and focus wouldn't clear and she couldn't remember any more, she couldn't *remember.*

"Shona?"

She blinked, and the waking world shuttered back into place. Cal was holding her arm a little too tightly, and she wondered, for a nerve-racking instant, what she had done this time; midway between the embankment wall and the road with its unending stream of traffic travelling too fast for a wet, murky night, Lambeth Bridge less than a stone's throw away. Had she broken towards one or the other, forgetting where she was, forgetting everything but the inner images and the memory of that voice…?

"You want to watch it in those shoes," Cal said. "Rain on top of all that dust and oil; makes the surface treacherous." He smiled, and the hand transferred from her arm to her opposite shoulder, squeezing, protective, proprietorial. "All right now?"

"Yes." Relief was an indescribable balm. She had only slipped, nothing worse, and she closed her eyes again to savour the pleasure of the moment. Strings of lights twinkling along the river, the distant, mournful hoot of a boat's siren, the roar and smell and warm, carbon-monoxide backdraught of the cars streaming by with their headlamps cutting swathes through the rain. Their hair and clothes were soaked, her impractical shoes were full of water; his coat, when she pressed her nose against it, smelled like a warm, wet and friendly dog. And it was good, so good. Good to exist, good to be here, *now*, good above all else to be with him.

Here. Now. She pushed all other concepts of time aside with determined savagery, and thought: *Just tonight. If there's any mercy in the world, just tonight.*

Cal's arm squeezed her again, pressing her tighter against the warm-dog fabric. "Where's it to be, then?"

"I... Ohh... I don't know. Anywhere." She laughed, turning her face up to the rain. They had tried on the off-chance to get a table at one of the floating restaurants, the converted Clyde steamer with the white paint, swaying gangplank and tiny lights in the dining-room ceiling. But the place had been full on Friday; they should have known, Cal said, and now they were footloose, hungry and with no particular direction in mind.

"McDonald's," Shona said and laughed again.

"God, you Philistine! No, look; we'll get a taxi and find somewhere in the West End, yes?"

"Yes." Anything. Anything that would let this night, this precious night, continue.

So there was satay and a bottle of wine in a Thai restaurant that gradually filled up with post-theatre diners cursing the weather and discussing the shows, and intermittent ice-white flashes as a table for eight celebrated someone's birthday and an inept but resolute member of the party took photos. Shona picked at the food, practising the knack, long perfected, of appearing to eat whilst foisting most of the dishes' contents on to Cal's plate. And over coffee that looked and tasted like old engine oil, Cal said, "You're coming back, aren't you?"

Everything within her said *yes, yes;* but for a moment she hesitated, waiting, alert for the inner warning signal that would mean she must shake her head and let him go through the charade of seeing her home, taking her to the hostel entrance, stealing one last kiss before the night carried him away. But the signal didn't come. This time, all was well.

She made the pretence, as she always did, of arguing about the bill and trying to insist that she should at least pay a share. But she knew that, as he always did, Cal would utterly refuse to take a single one of the pennies she didn't possess. They left, ducking under the awning that dripped huge, wet tears on the unsuspecting, walked to the bus stop, held each other and laughed like self-conscious children until the steamy, lit-up night service bus came to bear them away to Camden and Cal's flat. And there, between the shelf of engineering textbooks and the Save the Rainforest poster, in the bed on which he had carefully changed the sheets (and teased her again about hospital corners) there was the heat and the intimacy and the silent communion that Shona tried again and again to convince herself was not love, but which she knew could have no other name.

When Cal slept at last, hair and skin damp, snoring just a little, she stared into the dark at the silhouettes in the cramped room which grew more familiar every time.

And felt the breathing, the pulsing. In, out. In, out. Walls, the cavities of a straining heart. In, out. Reaching danger point. The bleeping of an alarm, followed by a long, indifferent, electronic tone that said, *too late*. Blood somewhere, but at a great remove and no longer relevant. Stillness. Hushed voices; someone swearing softly. A swing door, hissing on pneumatic hinges as someone else went out or came in. A sigh.

And a hand, reaching out of the suddenly silent dark, to touch her brow with long, rough-edged fingernails. And the voice.

Yes, Shona.

"No. Not tonight."

Not tonight. But soon. Soon.

"Please..." She flung herself up like someone held struggling under water then suddenly and unexpectedly released, and the hiss of her breath seemed shockingly loud. Cal mumbled, snorted and turned over, flinging one arm loosely across her stomach. Wanting to grasp his hand and kiss it, she forced herself instead to push it aside, and slid out of the bed. Clothes: bra, pants, tights, dress, she had looked good tonight, he had told her so at least half a dozen times. The impractical shoes. Coat. Bag. Nothing in it but a hairbrush, which she flicked through her hair without the aid of a mirror. Lastly, (wisdom protested, but she had to do it, *had* to), a note. Even Cal's bedroom was littered with paper; technical notes, calculations, letters from his family in Inverness, half-finished letters back. She pulled a sheet from a notepad with only a few doodles of cats on it, found a biro and hunched over the small, cluttered table.

> *Couldn't bear to wake you.*
> *My shift starts early; have to be back*
> *in good time or Sister B.*
> *will have me consigned to hell as a*
> *Scarlet Woman. Tomorrow?*
> *I'll phone.*
> *Love you.*
> *Shona.*

Tomorrow? She shouldn't have said it, but she had to. She *had* to. A quick glance towards the window; just the sound of an occasional car on the main road now, and the swish of the rain. She didn't know the time, but it didn't matter. She had nothing to fear from the streets. And the lie would be perpetuated, and the illusion maintained.

She closed the front door quietly, and there were no eyes to see her vanish into the night.

※ ※ ※

Shona knew the route well, the back streets, the brighter thoroughfares still noisy with traffic, though the cars had largely given way to delivery trucks, newspaper vans, the occasional patrolling police car with its bored occupants. No one accosted her; no one appeared even to notice her. She passed a few down-and-outs who shuffled between steel-meshed shop doorways, mumbling through cardboard boxes and plastic refuse sacks piled ready for the next collection, their minds half in the real world and half in another, more private hell. One old man looked up with a start as she hurried by. She glimpsed a dirty frizz of Celtic hair, eyes which might once have been sea-blue but were now rheumy and bloodshot and unable to focus; a broken-toothed mouth, dribbling, and for a moment his face registered a glimmer of shocked intelligence, as if an old racial memory had awoken. Then she was gone, unconcerned with him, and he returned to his rummaging and mumbling as her fleeting image faded from sight and thence from memory.

More streets, more wet pavements. She was soaked through now but didn't care; barely noticed. At last, in a dim backwater where tall, silent warehouses blocked the roar of the busy night, there were the lights of the hospital windows, chilly eyes in a high, blank wall of a face, and beyond them the gates and the weathered board at the entrance to the nurses' home.

The home was older than the hospital it served; once an almshouse, it now provided bed and board for the lay members of staff who had not taken the veil and the vows of the Quiet Sisters of Charity. Shona did not know what had drawn her to associate herself with this shabby but proud little maternity hospital, but it had become, insofar as the word could ever apply to her, home. And in their prayers, perhaps, the good sisters might unknowingly remember her, even though they had never seen her face.

She passed the daunting, rusty gates of the nurses' home, passed under the cold twin lamps that glared down vigilantly throughout the night to expose the guilt of those who flouted the sisters' strict and puritanical curfew. Moved on to where another warehouse, unlit, unused, its future balanced between the developer's acumen and the demolition gang's iron ball, reared against the sulphurous cloud cover. A door rocked on rust-eaten hinges behind a half-hearted barricade of slats; with the ease of long practice she slid between two of the slats and slipped inside. Pitch dark and echoing emptiness that smelled of urine and mildew and dry rot waited for her beyond the door. She hovered a moment, looking out and back along the wet, silent street. Then the door shuddered back into place and only rain disturbed the stillness.

❈ ❈ ❈

In the dream she was stretching out arms that seemed constricted by some soft, muffling substance. And though she strained with all her strength, fought with all her will, the goal she sought was always just beyond her reach. She could hear a baby crying, and thought that she cried, too; that in the distorted way of dreams she and the unknown, unseen infant were one and the same. Then the hands came again, guiding her as they stroked her with their broken nails, and the voice spoke in her ear and in her mind, soothing and comforting and giving an outlet to the bitter anger that burned like white metal deep inside. And when she woke to the greasy overcast dawn, she knew that this dawn, this day, promised more than rain. This day was malignant. This day was foretold.

It has come, Shona. It has come.

She looked up, through the ragged shadows of broken floors and treacherous rafters, and the rage came like a hurricane, screaming through her in fearsome rebuttal. *I will not answer! I will not do it! My will is my own, and I shall do what I will!* And huge, welling, the final, silent shriek of defiance: *I WILL NOT BE COMMANDED!*

For a moment, nothing. Then the reply came, as calm as her defiance had been wild.

But you will. You must. You know you always must.

Her rage collapsed in the face of shrivelling fear, for she knew the voice, and she knew its purpose, and she knew its implacable strength. Her defiance was a sham. Her path was ordained; the Quiet Sisters of Charity couldn't help her; the fictional Sister Beatrice, whose wrath she pretended to fear, couldn't help her. Cal couldn't help her. Above all, not Cal. Not *Cal.*

She was a wraith, an urchin, huddled in her thin coat and running through the rain in search of a phone box. Plastered hair, sodden clothes, useless shoes turning her heels painfully as she stumbled, ignored by the morning crowds. *Warn him,* said a last vestige of the self-will to which she had pretended. *Warn him. Tell him. Or there's no hope.*

Cramming into a booth at last, gasping, her breath misting the glass, she pressed the receiver to her ear. The read-out flashed, asking for coins; she ignored it, stabbed the buttons, sensed the bypassing of the system and heard Cal's phone begin to ring. And ring, and ring. He'd left. An early lecture; now she remembered; and she smashed the handset down with helpless frustration. Don't cry. *Don't* cry. *Think.*

Away. The idea was a lifeline. If she was away from Cal, far away, then she couldn't do it. She could go away, and never come back. However great the loss, however painful the knowledge that he would never understand why she had gone, it would be better. It *must* be better.

She would go home. She couldn't remember how long it had been since she was there, but however much it might have changed it was a refuge, a familiar oasis. Yes. Certainty filled her, and with it a kind of peace. She would go home.

❂ ❂ ❂

Euston was glass and noise and an echoing concourse where station announcements boomed unintelligibly over a susurrant background of hurrying feet. For a long time Shona stood staring up at the departure board, watching times and destinations and platform numbers shuffle and rearrange themselves. Queues waited before the folding gates, shuffled forward, and were swallowed down sloping concrete throats to their trains. She watched the travellers, watched the board, and at last saw the name she had been waiting for. She read it three times to be certain, committing the time and the platform to memory, then turned and hurried through the zigzag of people to the ticket office. They called it the Travel Centre now. She wasn't yet used to that.

More queues. Ahead of her, four Scandinavians struggled with backpacks and a vast nylon holdall; they bumped her, apologised in smiling, careful English. At the ticket window they asked polite but complicated questions and had difficulty with the currency; Shona shuffled restless feet and tried not to shiver until at last, reading their tickets with intense and slightly puzzled interest, they manoeuvred their luggage out of the way and it was her turn.

She didn't know whether she actually asked for a single to Glasgow; she might have spoken the words or merely thought them.

But the clerk punched the terminal without even troubling to look up, and though she put nothing on the carousel his hand moved reflexively as though to scoop up notes or a credit card. The carousel jerked again and her ticket lay on the dull metal plate before her. She took it, and slid aside as a tall man in a dark coat, harassed and hurrying, breathlessly demanded Birmingham New Street.

She flexed the ticket in her palm. It felt peculiar; the wrong shape and the wrong size. Her passport out of Cal's life. She left the Travel Centre, looked around. Telephones. Perhaps by now he would have returned and be waiting for her call. She should tell him. It was only fair. And she wanted so much to hear his voice one last time.

The number rang and rang without an answer. Shona bit her lip hard and tried again in case it was a wrong connection, though she knew it wasn't. Ringing, ringing, and still no reply. Twenty minutes before the train left. Ten more and she would try again. In the event, and perhaps subconsciously aware of what she was doing and why, fifteen minutes passed before she dialled the number a third time. Four rings — then a click, and Cal's familiar, longed-for voice.

"Cal..."

"Shona. Hey, I'm sorry, have you been trying to call me? I got caught up at college; there was—"

"Cal, I'm going home." She cut across him baldly, bluntly. She had tried to rehearse the things she wanted to say, but now, hearing him, speaking to him, they had fled.,

There was a silence. Then. "Wh—"

"I'm sorry." She couldn't let him ask the questions. "I must, Cal. I can't explain. I just ... had to ring and say goodbye. Maybe I shouldn't have, but ... I had to."

"Shona!" Bewildered panic in Cal's voice. "Shona, wait, what are you telling me? What do you mean, home? What's going on?"

"Please." The word sounded ugly, distorted by tears. "I have to go. I have to leave. I *have* to. But..." *I love you.* She wanted to say it but couldn't. "Cal... take care. And please, try not to be angry with me." *I love you.*

"Where are you? Tell me! I don't understand... Shona, for Christ's sake—"

I love you. "Take care, Cal. Goodbye."

She stared at the replaced handset for a long time. Long enough to know instinctively that the train had gone without her. It didn't matter. There would be another.

And later, much later, on the platform at last and climbing on board the train through one of the open carriage doors, she knew what she had tried to do and was thankful that she had failed. Weakness, foolishness. She should have been stronger and not called him. She had known better, but she hadn't done better. But it didn't matter. Now, now that she was leaving, it didn't matter any more.

❋ ❋ ❋

There was a creaking lurch as the train moved off. Then long minutes of cautious, rocking progress as it slowly negotiated its way through the spaghetti of converging lines, goods yards and overhead cables that formed the suburbs of Euston's city within the city. At last they began to gather speed as the train finally escaped London's net. Shona had found a place in a near-empty carriage, and sat hunched against the window, leaning away from the aisle and grateful for the empty seats immediately around her. Outside, wisps of smoky cloud scudded alongside the train under the bloated belly of the overcast sky; occasional bursts of rain spattered against the window, as though someone had thrown a bucket of water at the glass. Above and below, the lines and their parallel power cables hummed mesmerically past; inside, the carriage was warm and well lit, and the hypnotic thrum of power and the bogies was a familiar lullaby. Shona's father had worked on the railway; as a little child she had known the north-western routes well, though that was in the days before diesel, let alone electricity, had come to rule. She had had a record, she remembered, one she loved to play on the old gramophone. *Coronation Scot.* The rhythm of a train, running, racing, powering north into the thundering dark, carrying her home. Humming the tune silently in her mind, and trying to make it run in time with the rocking of the carriage, she closed her eyes, smiling in a semi-doze.

Until a presence, intruding, slid into the seat opposite hers and her eyes flicked open.

"Shona." His face was haggard, eyes wild with a painful mixture of fear and relief.

She stared at him, and realised what she had done.

Cal reached over the formica table and gripped her hands before she could pull them away. "Shona, thank God I—"

"How did you know?" Her voice was a frightened whisper.

"I rang the hospital, Shona." Now there was accusation as well as the other emotions, and she saw that he was as afraid as she was, though for a very different reason. His fingers tightened, and they hurt. "There's no nurse there called Shona Wilson, and no such person as Sister Beatrice. Shona, why have you been lying to me? What's going on?"

She couldn't speak. She could only stare at him, her brain fighting between the onslaughts of horror and gladness. He had followed her. Knowing she was playing with fire, she hadn't been able to stop herself from testing him, and he had passed the test. He loved her enough not to let her go.

"You..." Her voice caught she licked her lips. She was shaking now. "You shouldn't have called them."

"What did you expect me to do?" His fear was finding an outlet in anger. "When you tell me out of the blue that you're going, and you won't tell me why, and—" Heads turned further along the carriage; Cal stopped, then lowered his voice. "Did you think I was just going to let you go, and that'd be the end of it?"

She looked away. "I don't know."

"Jesus *Christ*!" He pulled his hands away, running them through his hair in helpless frustration, then with an effort pulled himself together. "Shona." Gentle now, the anger subsided. "I've been trying to understand, and I can't. Why did you lie about where you lived and what you did? Why couldn't you tell me the truth, whatever it is?"

She shook her head, mute, and he clenched his hands together on the table top, knuckles white. "If something's wrong, something in your life, you've got to tell me about it. *Please*."

"No."

Another pause. "Is it to do with your family? You're not ... married, are you? Is that it?"

She laughed, harshly and without humour, shaking her head again.

"What, then? Shona, for Christ's sake, it's sheer chance that I got on the same train as you, but if I hadn't, I'd have gone to Glasgow anyway; I'd have followed you—"

"You don't know whereabouts I live."

"Then I'd have walked the streets until I found out! Damn it, don't you understand what I'm trying to say? Don't you understand how much you mean to me?"

She did now; now that it was too late. "Yes..."

"Don't I mean anything to you?"

"Oh, yes." Shona's eyes brimmed with tears. "Yes, Cal."

"Then—"

"*No!*" And she flung herself out of the seat, lurching into the aisle, staggering and swaying towards the connecting door. Cal shouted her name and came after her, but she had a head start. She stumbled through the door that obligingly opened, turned sharply, rushed into the toilet and slammed its door at her back, locking it and leaning hard against it. She was panting, crying, trying to keep silent as she heard him outside.

"Shona." The handle rattled. "Shona!"

Go away, go away.

"Shona, I know you're there. For God's sake—"

"Go away!" she shouted, thumping the door with her fist. "Get off when the train stops, go back to London and leave me alone! Cal, *please!* Just *do* it!"

There was a long pause. Then: "Okay. I'm going to count to five, and if you haven't come out I'm going to bust the door open. All right?" His voice was sweet reason, and she knew he meant it. "And I don't care if I do get had up in court for criminal damage. This is more important. One."

Go away.

"Two."

Please. For your own sake.

"Three."

The train was slowing down. They were approaching a station. Cal wasn't going to listen to her; maybe, she thought wildly, she could break away, jump off the train, just run. *For his sake.*

"Four."

The lock clicked. Slowly, Shona opened the door.

For a moment they stood staring at each other. Disembarking passengers were already crowding out into the gangway between the carriages; beyond the door the shapes of industrial buildings, indistinct in gathering dusk, skimmed past as the train continued to slow. People stared curiously at them but they paid no heed. Cal was breathing hard with the adrenalin that had been building in him; now the pent energy had nowhere to go, and for one second he was unsure of himself, and vulnerable. Shona took her chance and shot out of the cramped cubbyhole like a rabbit out of a burrow. She knew she was behaving insanely, but she no longer cared; fear for him had taken her beyond reason. She pushed violently between two women, trod on a foot, heard an indignant shout of protest, and flung herself at the carriage door, clawing at the stiff and heavy catch as she tried to pull it open.

"Stop that! It's still going too fast, it—"

"Shona!"

"What's that stupid bitch doing—"

"SHONA!" And Cal had her arm even as the heavy door swung open with a thump and a sucking rush of cold air. Someone yelled, Shona twisted around and tried to pull Cal away, collided with a heavy body, lost her balance. She felt her feet going from under her, and her legs tangled with Cal's as she struck the grimy floor —

And the shouts of horror, the shock and panic and scramble and grinding lurch of brakes as someone pulled the communication cord, rose up like a tidal wave against her reeling senses, freezing into that one final image of Cal's terrified face, as he lost his hold on the man who tried to save him, and fell screaming from the train.

❈ ❈ ❈

Instinct had guided her as surely as a moth was drawn to the light

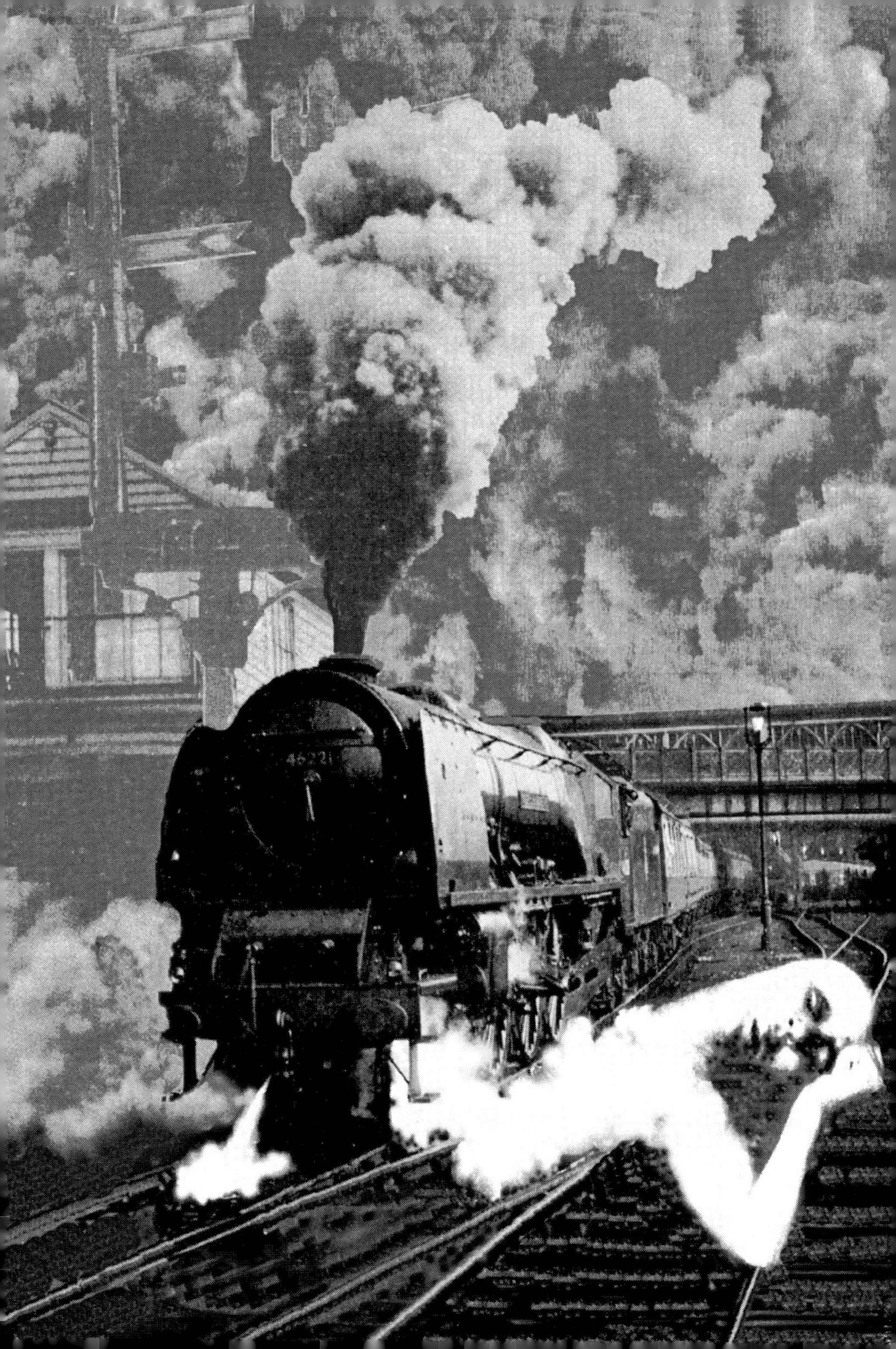

of fire, and she stood in the open space in front of the main building, by an ugly spotlit fountain that played into a tile-rimmed and sterile pool. From a place where no one would find her she had watched the lights and the milling people in the dark, heard the ambulance and police sirens, seen the stabbing beams and the uniformed men and the paramedics and the garish, orange and white vehicle that took Cal away. Then she had turned her back and walked, leaving the crowd and the chaos, into the city and to the place where she had to be. Now, under a sky made sulphurous by city lights, she stared at the wide glass doors and the bright, separate world beyond them; not her world now, but alien. Rows of lights from a hundred windows. Cars parked on the forecourt. Another ambulance arriving, but unhurried; no emergency this time. She could smell, or imagine she smelled, that sharp hospital scent; the building seemed to exhale it. And somewhere, she knew where, she knew which window, was Cal, and the people who were trying to save him.

This wasn't her hospital. Hers had been at home in Glasgow, far away in both time and distance. Tiled and antiseptic and always rushing, strip lighting and rattling trolleys, masks and gloves and fearful faces, and pain, and blood, then a baby crying in the dark and the first touch of the hands that had reached out of the dark to claim her in death and show her what she must now become. She had seen her man's stricken face, though she couldn't now remember his name. But she had never seen her child. And that was then, and this was now, and the voice was speaking to her, speaking gently in her mind.

Yes, Shona. Yes.

The hospital's glass doors hissed open and two nurses came out, hunching their shoulders against the wind's bite and hurrying across the forecourt. Shona didn't look at them: she was staring up at one window among the many, and as she stared she pushed back the folds of the garment that covered her, letting it slide from her shoulders, down her torso, over hips and thighs, to fall in a grey, crumpled mass at her feet. Naked, she gazed at the window as the nurses passed on the far side of the fountain. Their chattering voices were thin in the chill night; she was invisible to them now, invisible to them all. All but one.

As she bent to gather the crumpled linen, her hair fell about her face, its long strands were like tendrils of trailing weed dredged from ponds, from rivers, from dark water where forces older and colder than the stark, bright civilisation around her ran like blood through the arteries of the land. Like blood ... the stains on the shroud were old and rust-brown now as she let it fall into the fountain pool, watched it swirl in the water like a dead woman's hair.

She might have given in and let him follow her all the way home. Perhaps that would have been more fitting; to be in Scotland where the old beliefs were still a little closer to the surface. Or she might have stayed in London; might have accepted the inevitable from the first, rather than try to change what would be. Instead, by an indifferent quirk of chance, it had ended here, in a city unfamiliar to them both, in a place where they had no roots and no memories. It didn't matter. It was all one, now.

She gazed up to the window, to the room where light and warmth and quiet voices pervaded, where the monitors and the machines were recording the failing spark of life, and her lips, clay-cold, chalk-white, formed a word.

"Cal-um." Out of a dark more primal than the city night, like the cry of an owl heard on the wind, a whisper in a shunned place, a moaning from the haunted sea.

"Cal-um." She called to him, cried his name in lonely mourning, summoned him home. And in the pool's cold illumination, under the tumbling stream of the fountain, her dead hands worked among the folds of linen, working at the old, old blood that could never be erased, washing, and washing, and washing.

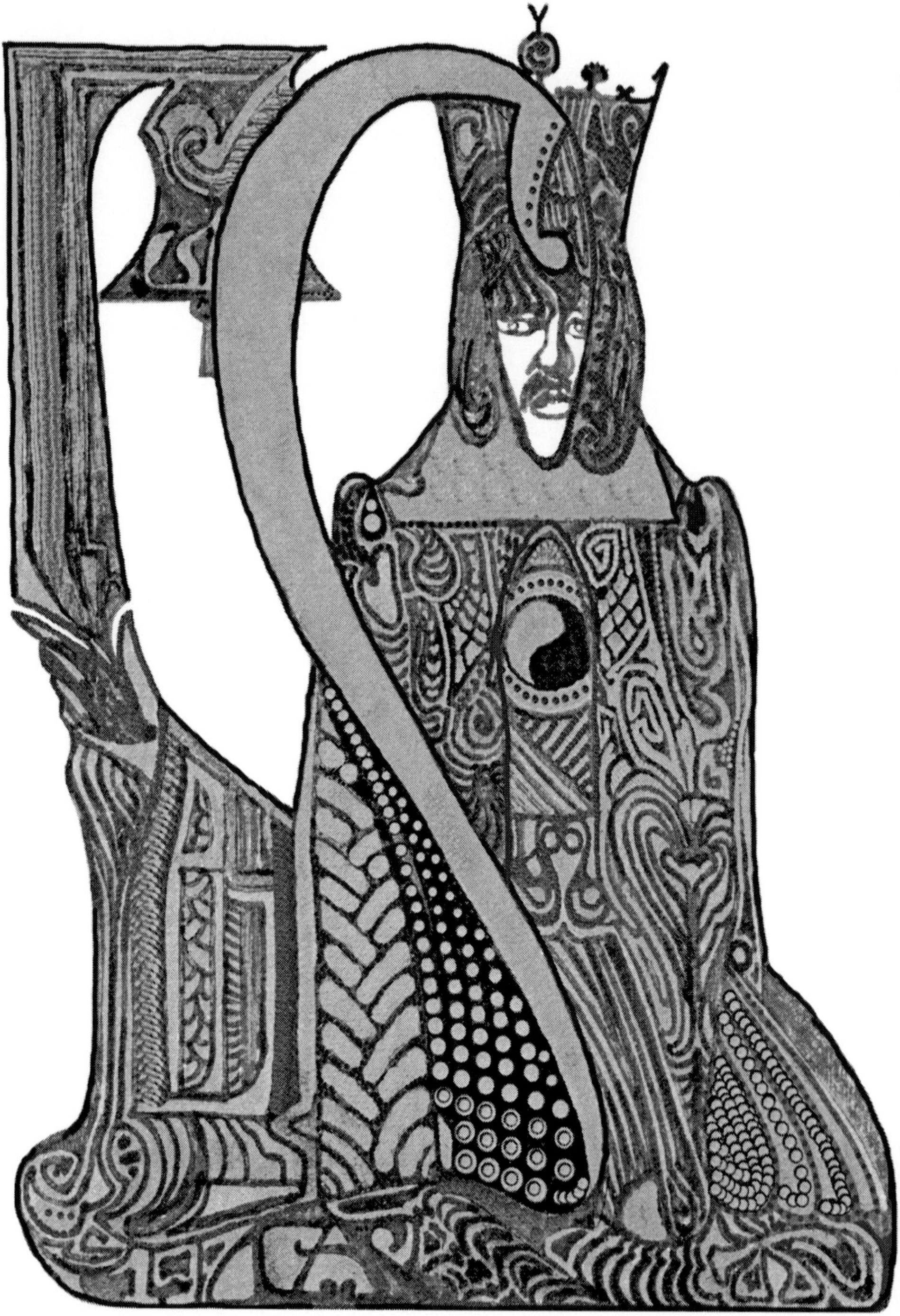

THE SPIRAL GARDEN

The chancellor entered the audience room, bowed, and said, "Your majesty. The queen is definitely with child."

Eyes shifted, faces showed cautious animation, as the inner coterie of courtiers applied their well practised art of looking without appearing to look at the king. In their midst, framed by a shaft of late sunlight that created the illusion of a halo around his figure, their royal master turned his head and for some moments regarded the chancellor with sombre consideration. Then he nodded. He did not speak.

The knot of courtiers parted, forming an aisle to the ornately carved doors, which at a hasty signal from the chancellor were flung fully open by the guardsmen outside. Pikes clashed in salute; the king ignored them, ignored all in his path, and left the chamber with the chancellor diligent at his heels. As the doors closed again, one courtier, who was young and naive and thus not yet fully *au fait* with this yearly ritual and its significance, cast a curious glance towards the window where the king had been standing. He asked, though not aloud, what his monarch found compelling in the vista outside, that it had absorbed him so deeply through the hours of waiting. It was only a garden. And the king did not even like flowers. Not that there were any flowers at this time of year; with winter still biting down on the world the only things blossoming in the garden were a series of stone carvings, each in the shape of a spiral tapering heavenwards, all but one, which was larger but to all intents identical in every way. Stone spirals, set between the formal box hedges like giant, incongruous sea-shells. The young courtier was aware of what they symbolised, of course. Remembrance; memorials to souls that had risen from this world and joined the gods in eternal bliss. But this was a time of rejoicing, not an occasion to dwell on death, and the king's preoccupation puzzled him.

He shrugged his shoulders, unaware even that he did so, and returned his attention to less taxing matters. Across the room, one of his seniors with enough years and experience to understand and pity the naivety of youth, observed the unconscious gesture and smiled ironically. The boy would learn a few lessons over the months to come, he thought. Each year it was the same. And if the pattern was repeated yet again, as he suspected it would be, there would be a few older heads on young shoulders by the time autumn came once more.

Though the palace corridors were much used at this time of day, the king acknowledged no one as he stalked, with his chancellor still behind him, towards the Tower of Contemplation. The Tower had been named some centuries ago, with more than a touch of irony; for in the past it had been the residence, often the final residence, of felons who had considered themselves more fit to rule than their anointed monarch.

"Contemplation" had been another word for "Repentance", and those who failed to repent within a given time had taken their last walk from the tower's confines to the headsman's block. These days there was less call for such drastic measures; the royal dynasty had been established for two centuries and few were foolish enough, or even discontented enough, to oppose it. But the tower and its title remained. Now it had a new, if temporary, function.

King and chancellor turned aside from the main corridors and into a long narrow passage where there were no torches to augment the thin winter light. The passage turned twice, sharply, then there was a single, straight run before them, which ended at a locked and guarded door.

The king saw with arid satisfaction that his instructions had been followed to the letter. The two guards at the door were female, hard-eyed and incorruptible and armed with sabres which they could and would use without compunction if the need arose. Between them, pacing the floor nervously and fingering the sash that proclaimed his rank and profession, was his personal physician.

"My liege," The physician made an elaborate bow. The guards stared stonily ahead, trained to ignore their master until and unless he should require otherwise.

The king's cold gaze raked over the physician, and he said without preamble, "It is true?"

"It is true, Sire." Another bow; the physician's skullcap almost fell off and he snatched it undignifiedly back into place. "I completed the examination of Her Grace's person minutes ago, and the symptoms are beyond doubt."

"Good." The physician was not a married man, the king knew. His preferences tended in other directions, which was why he had been appointed to this task. "And a date?" the king added.

"It's impossible to be absolute in these things, of course, Sire; but I would anticipate the likely parturition at or around Hunter's-feast."

The king nodded. Easy enough, then, to calculate the day of the conception. He was satisfied, thus far. "Very well." He made an imperious gesture to the guards. "Unlock the door."

The women snapped to attention; a key was inserted, grated in the lock, and the king entered the tower. For a moment, forgetting the circumstances, the chancellor made as if to follow, but a sabre moved smoothly and significantly to bar the way and he hastily withdrew. His gaze met that of the physician; they shared an uneasy, almost sympathetic look. The door closed, and without the need to exchange a word the two men walked quietly away down the corridor.

❂ ❂ ❂

The tower had two rooms, one above the other. The queen was housed in the uppermost, and was sitting by the window and staring out at the bright but chilly afternoon. She looked up when the king entered, and though her face betrayed no emotion, nor any clue to her thoughts, her grey eyes were steady as they regarded him. She was his second wife, much younger and considerably more beautiful than the first, who had died twenty years ago whilst attempting, unsuccessfully, to give birth to a live child. The king had not loved his first wife and, on one level, had little more interest in his second. But on another level, the new queen – though after two decades of marriage it was, perhaps, time for the "new" epithet to be set aside – was an intense and almost obsessive focus for his attention. For neither the king nor his spouse was growing any younger. Time was running short for them both. This time, the monarch was implacably resolved that nothing should go wrong.

"The physician tells me," he said, "that you are with child."

The fire crackled peaceably. The queen continued to gaze back at him. "Yes, my lord."

"He also tells me that the birth will take place at the time of Hunter's-Feast." A pause. "The likely date of conception corresponds acceptably enough."

Her cheeks flushed slightly and now she did turn away, so that he could not see her expression. "Yes," she said again.

Silence fell for several seconds. Then: "Your needs are fully attended to?"

"Yes. Thank you."

"If there is anything you require, your lady in waiting may relay a request to me. But only to me." She said something under her breath, and his brows knitted frowningly together. "What? There is something you want?"

The queen drew a sharp, quick breath and said, "Only a measure of freedom, my lord. Freedom to walk in the garden—"

The king said, "Ha!" Nothing more; just a single, clipped sound that in itself was an absolute refusal. The queen fell silent and turned back to the window, and for a few moments he stood motionless, watching her with the blend of resentment, suspicion and desire that he always felt in her company. Desire must be held in abeyance now, until her term was over. Resentment was an old companion, and of no importance. And suspicion... Well, he had done all that any human agency could do to see that there could be no grounds, no chance for doubt to flourish. Time, now, would be the only arbiter. If all went according to the plan he had so carefully laid, when summer gave way to autumn he would have a living heir.

He would have a living heir.

The queen still gazed out of the window. To him her face was inscrutable, though to anyone who had taken more trouble than he to know her well, some trace of her innermost thoughts reflected in a faint, bleak cast to her far-focused eyes. The king made a rough sound in his throat, part farewell and part threat. Then he left the room, taking care to lock the door behind him, and walked down the stairs to the guards and the corridor and the continuing business of his kingdom.

❋ ❋ ❋

The queen's lady in waiting came to her, as always, at sunset. She brought a supper designed by the physician to promote a high degree of health and strength, and watched as her mistress dutifully ate every morsel. Then she helped the queen to disrobe, changing her russet day-gown with its ermine trimming for a white silk night-shift and grey woollen shawl threaded with silver. She combed out her mistress's long, dark hair, put soft slippers on her feet, and tied around her head the white matron's bonnet that would keep her head warm as she slept. Then she made up the fire, turned down the curtained bed and, unspeaking — for what was the point in speaking when the queen so rarely answered? — returned to her own chamber on the level below.

The queen did not go to bed immediately. She snuffed out her candles, knowing that eyes would be watching the tower from other parts of the palace, then returned to her customary place at the window and sat down once more.

The last of the sun was gone, and only a faint stain of colour remained in the upper part of the sky. The night promised to be clear; soon the stars would show, and the vista on which she gazed would take on the darker, stranger aspect that she had learned to love. The garden. Her garden.

She stared down at the formal pattern of hedges and gravel walks that formed a dimming mosaic in the dusk and, as she did each evening and morning and at other hours between, counted the spiral sculptures that showed pale against the darkening green. Twenty-six. One for each year of her own wedded life, six for the years of the first queen's truncated reign, and the single, larger monument that commemorated the former queen herself. Would there be a twenty-seventh? The court, those who knew at least a part of the truth, would pray daily that the number would not increase again. And the very, very few who knew the whole truth would not pray but would only watch, though they would take great care to keep their unease to themselves.

While she... The queen's fine mouth tightened just a little, and the moue made her look suddenly old beyond her years. Which perhaps she was, for though her knowledge of the wider world was small, what she had experienced throughout her marriage more than made up for her innocence of the broader canvas.

She closed her eyes suddenly as the most recent of those experiences rose in her memory. The moon had turned twice since that night just after Frost-Feast, but the ugliness, the brutality of it was still sharp in her mind, despite the fact that the indignity and humiliation were nothing new. There had been a banquet in the great hall, which she was not permitted to attend, and half way through the evening the king had sent word to the tower that she was to expect him an hour after midnight. Her lady in waiting had come; in silence the queen had changed her clothes and dressed her hair, and at the appointed time she had heard her lord approaching, accompanied by several of his more raucous courtiers. The courtiers were singing ribald songs whose words turned her stomach as she listened to them, and they had trampled through the spiral garden like pigs let loose in an orchard, shouting their own and their master's prowess to the indifferent night sky.

The king, though, was not drunk. Not entirely sober, but still in complete and glacial control of himself and his intentions. He was, she reflected, never anything less than that. He had climbed the stairs alone, he had entered this room, and without greeting or preamble had said, curtly, "You are ready?" She had looked away; it was consent enough and he stripped off surcoat and breeches and pushed her down on the bed. Her shrinking pain when he pinched and bit her breasts was enough to arouse him, and he took her forcibly and without a trace of tenderness or even the interest that a cruel lover might have taken in pleasuring himself at her expense. She endured, as she always did, and when it was done he had left her in the bed and sat in her place at the window, from where he could look at the antics of his sycophants who now were crudely serenading them both and inflicting more damage on the garden.

He had stayed for three hours, performed his duty on her three times, then left her with the parting comment that if there was anything she required her lady in waiting might relay a request to him, but only to him. The queen had lain as he left her, eyes focused on the canopy overhead but seeing nothing, ears soiled by the noise of the celebrating courtiers outside. Then when the revellers had been rejoined by their master and had at last gone away back to the banquet to celebrate their triumph, she had sat up and, with practised expertise, made herself vomit into a bronze bowl set ready on her bedside table. In practice it achieved nothing; in principle it cleansed just a little of the taint she felt on her soul. Then, she had cried herself to sleep.

So: again the night and the time and the auguries had been carefully calculated, and again the royal seed had germinated within the garden of her body. She was with child. For the twentieth time the king was to have an heir. And this time, for the first time, the queen would not need to pray for her husband's sanity when her time of deliverance came. This time, there was no room for doubt. This time, the child would live.

❈ ❈ ❈

Three more months passed, and spring came to the world. It arrived with a blasting roar of a gale that uprooted trees, snatched away precarious roofs and shook the Tower of Contemplation to its foundations; but there was a silver lining to the wind, for it also brought rain and warm air to drive out the last of winter's frosts. On its heels came softness, mildness, stillness. The young shoots that had cowered under the onslaught took confidence and began to grow. Hibernating animals dared, at last, to show themselves. And the new life in the queen's womb was growing.

The physician examined his patient every few days and reported each result to the king. All was satisfactory. The child was developing as it should. The king, who had repeatedly checked and re-checked his calculations and found no possible fault with them even by his exacting standards, began to unbend a little in his attitude towards his wife. Possibly the burgeoning season had some mellowing effect on his nature, or possibly it was simply that the cold inner voice of doubt was losing its grip. He took to visiting her more often, staying to talk for a while and now and then even bringing some small gift that he thought would please her. Once or twice he even smiled at her. And one afternoon, when the sun warmed the tower room and relieved its grimness a little, he agreed to her request that she might walk for a while in the spiral garden.

He did not, of course, permit her to go alone, but accompanied her himself. After months of close confinement the queen was unused to exercise, and that combined with the thickening of her body made her ungainly in her movements. The king quashed his annoyance at this imperfection and concentrated instead on the play of light in her hair as, stiffly and formally, they paced together along the paths and between the neat green edgings, tracing out the pattern that a careful gardener had laid down decades before either of them was born. The queen did not converse, and answered her husband's few remarks only with a nod or a smile or, at best, a "yes," or "no." But she looked, hungrily and with a peculiar air of distraction, at everything the garden displayed, as though seeing it with the new eyes of one just delivered from blindness. And at nineteen of the stone spirals she paused and murmured a name under her breath. A sad little list, like a litany. The King knew whose names they were, and felt the stirrings of a dark, angry demon in the depths of his mind, for he did not wish to be reminded of what was past, and literally and metaphorically, buried. But although he could have silenced her with one command, he stayed his tongue. Women in her condition had strange fads and fancies; if she wished to utter the names of her dead children it was doubtless merely her own talisman, a conciliatory gesture to ward off yet another misfortune. So he closed his ears to her quiet recitation, and looked beyond the garden wall to the main wing of the palace, and speculated contentedly enough about nurses and toys and suites of rooms and tutors and all the other trappings that his heir, his living heir, would need as he grew.

They completed one circuit of the garden, then the queen said respectfully that she had had her fill of walking. She felt tired and, with her lord's gracious permission, would like now to return to her tower and rest. The king looked at her with a mixture of alarm and suspicion, but his momentary fear that she might have over-exerted herself and damaged the child was swiftly quelled. She showed no signs of strain or discomfort; in fact her demeanour was calmer than he could remember having seen it in many a year. She looked serene, and, relieved, he turned without a word and led the way back to her prison and the waiting, impassive guards.

He did not come up to her room with her, and as she climbed the stairs with her lady in waiting in solicitous attendance the queen gave mute thanks for that. It was bad enough to be forced to endure his presence in the garden that meant so much to her, without the added insult of having him linger here through some warped sense of duty. Or suspicion. When she asked to retire she had seen the look in his eyes before he could mask it, and it only made her despise him the more. A savage observation came to her tongue, and involuntarily she whispered it to the stairwell: "You could have had your precious heir a long, long time ago. That choice was yours."

The lady in waiting, who had heard her voice but not her words, paused and said, "Madam?"

The queen made a cancelling gesture, indicating that it was something of no moment and to be ignored. The lady in waiting was well-trained enough to forget what she should not remember, and so they continued on in silence.

Reaching her room the queen dismissed the lady, saying that she meant to sleep and did not wish to be woken until the next designated mealtime. The door closed with quiet tact, and as the woman's footsteps diminished back down the stairs the queen did not, as usual, move either to the window seat or to her bed. Instead, she manoeuvred herself awkwardly to her knees by the hearth, and her fingers prised at one of the smaller hearth stones, cool now that the kindly weather had made a fire unnecessary. The stone lifted, revealing a hollow chamber between the rafters of the room below, and the queen reached inside and drew out a small bundle, wrapped against dirt and decay in an oiled silk pouch. No other living soul had set eyes on this pouch and its contents, or even knew of its existence. The only other soul who had known of it — and, in fact, had procured it for her — had died shortly after the birth of the queen's last child. Or rather, had been executed on a trumped-up charge that no justice in the land would have accepted as valid. But the king was above justice, and the life of a servant, even the queen's servant, counted for nothing against the greater issue that had been at stake.

The queen unrolled the pouch. Inside were papers, written upon in black ink, in a meticulous hand. Words, and diagrams. They were very old, and she had never inquired how her late lady in waiting had come by them, for some questions were better left unanswered. But when the lady had died, and the queen's newborn son had died – the fourteenth boy; those who had arranged the royal match had predicted that her body would predominantly produce male children, and they had been right – she had finally found the courage to make the decision that she knew in her heart should have been made a long time ago. The decision to take matters into her own hands. The decision to rebel.

And the decision to claim vengeance for nineteen innocent souls.

She knew the summoning words by heart, but still she read them again just to be sure that there would be no mistake, for mistakes, as her former lady had warned her, could bring disaster. The language was half familiar, for it was the old tongue of the land, which passing centuries had changed and corrupted, and in her mind she ran silently through the peculiar pronunciations and oddities of dialect until she was sure that she would not falter. Or, if she did, that her faltering would be through fear and not through incompetence. After all, there was always fear in matters such as this. It was a part – albeit a small part – of the price that must be paid. But that price, all of it, was well worth the paying, for there was nothing else left to her now.

The tower room was quiet. Outside the sun was westering, and the shadows of the stone spirals in the garden stretched across the paths and flowerbeds like fingers pointing to her window. Slowly, softly, calmly, and with something in her voice that carried an uneasy undertone of reluctant yet impassioned desire, the queen began to speak the words of summoning.

❖ ❖ ❖

It did not happen until full darkness came. She had expected that, and patience was a virtue with which she was long familiar. For form's sake she had lit a candle in her window, as she always did, and she sat upon the bed, face quiet, body quiet, waiting.

A small sound, like the crackle of a distant fire, heralded his arrival. The queen looked up, and was in time to see the dim, dark shape of him materialise beside the empty hearth. She heard his breathing, heavy, like the breath of some large animal. She saw the coarse mane of red-gold hair that framed his face and grew, too, over the massive shoulders and bulky arms and down the sharp-spined curve of his back. And she saw his eyes that glowed like live coals, and his full-mouthed, contented, lascivious smile.

He said, in the hoarse voice that she remembered: "Woman. Why have you called me again?"

Sickness churned in the queen's stomach, but she knew its cause and thrust the thought of it away. Her eyes met those of the demon, her demon, and she replied, "To be certain. To know that there can be no room for doubt."

He laughed, lazily. "You grow like your husband."

"No. I simply wish to reassure myself that our bargain stands."

"Oh, yes." She heard him shift his bulk a little, and the small sound both excited and repelled her. "Oh, yes, woman. It stands."

"My child will live."

"Your child grows, and it is healthy, and all is well."

"A boy."

The visitor inclined his head.

"And he will resemble the king."

Another soft laugh. "More than any who were born and died before him. More than the king's true children. You know I have that power."

She did; and even as it eased her heart it also sent a shaft of memory thrilling through her. The demon read what was in her mind, and his banked-ember eyes grew momentarily hotter, sharing the recollection.

To calm herself, and distract from the inner surge, she said, "I hate him."

"Of course. Or you would not have turned to me."

"Oh, I would. For I..." But she stopped then, realising what she had been about to say; realising the depth of the misery and frustration and thwarted yearnings that she had suffered for so many years.

He spoke the words where she could not. "For with me, there was another reward. With me, you knew pleasure for the first and only time in your life."

She couldn't deny it. She hung her head.

"Don't be ashamed," he said, almost gently; though such a being, she knew, could have no true compassion. "Why should you not also find pleasure in your search for retribution?" That unhuman smile widened. "And it was only once. It can only ever be once."

"I wish..."

"Ah, *wishes*. Your greatest and deepest wish has been granted; be content with that." He held out one hand; for an irrational moment she thought he meant to take her fingers in his and hold them, but then she saw the truth, saw the small, tightly-rolled parchment that he displayed to her. A spot of blood — her blood — stained one corner. She could not see the other marks, made when she had opened her own vein; the words, the promise, the pledge. But she remembered every syllable that she had written.

"Yes," she said. "I understand. I am content."

There was another heavy, shifting sound as the demon rose to his feet. "Then, if you are reassured, I will leave you." A pause, and to the queen's hectic imagination the atmosphere in the room chilled suddenly and ominously. "If you're wise, you will not call on me again. I have many demands on my time, and to spend it in trivial matters does not please me."

A shiver went through her. "I am sorry. I will remember."

She sensed rather than saw him smile. "Next time," he said, "*I will summon you.*"

There was an untoward sound, like the boom of an old, slow gong somewhere far, far down in the palace's foundations. The queen blinked. When her vision cleared, the demon was gone.

She lay back on the bed, trying to quell the pounding of her heart. With his last words, the demon had reminded her sharply and emphatically of what she was to expect when her time came. All would be well with the birth; the child would be healthy, and it would resemble the king. But it would not be the king's child. Unlike the others, the others who had died, the others whose memorials she saw each day in her spiral garden, this last fruit of her womb would be no true heir to the kingdom, but something else. Something *else*. And for the sake of the vengeance she would wreak through its creation, she would give her soul, and rejoice in the giving.

Very softly, she laughed. On the surface it was gentle laughter, recalling the carefree girl she had once been before the deathly shrouds of the court enfolded her, and before she had come to understand the true depths of her husband's jealous insanity. But underlying it was an edge that, in its way, betrayed a mind as deranged as the king's. How could she not be deranged, she asked herself detachedly, to have made such a bargain as this? No matter, no matter. Better madness, and then death, than what a queen's life had to offer her in this accursed place. Better that, than to see yet another child die for the sake of her husband's suspicion and mistrust. This time, he had taken every step that was possible to ensure that, even in his twisted mind, there could be no grounds for doubt. This time, he had no fear that the fruit of her womb was not his. And this time, like every other time, he was wrong.

The queen rose to her feet, not graceful now; nor ever graceful again, she thought; at least not in life. Afterwards... well, who could say? Not she. She would discover, when the time came. Whatever it was, whatever fate awaited her, it would be worthwhile. She walked to the window and looked out over the garden. The moon had risen, and its light etched the stone spirals in sharp relief against the softer contours of the bushes and flowers. Summer was approaching in earnest now. Summer, then autumn. The first queen had died in autumn, she recalled. She herself had been sixteen then, hardly more than a child, but she remembered the dreary days of official mourning that had continued until Frost-Feast. A month later, the king's eye had fallen on her, and she had gone bewilderedly to the marriage altar and the marriage bed, to achieve for him what his late wife could not. Narrowing her eyes, she looked with sudden intentness at the single, larger spiral among the cluster of stones, and wondered if her predecessor knew of her and her story. It had been different for the first queen, of course. All her children had died and shrivelled within her, even the last one that had sent her to the grave in her turn. There had been no question of their legitimacy. No question of infidelity or intrigue or deceit.

"But I was beautiful." She spoke aloud, though very softly, as if she were sharing a private confidence with the woman whom she had never met. "That was the difference. That was why he did not trust. He denied it; oh yes, he did, and he would deny it still, if anyone had the courage to ask him. But no one asks, not now. No one dares. He is mad, you see. Mad and sick and ... evil. And am I evil? Perhaps. But if I am, it is no less than he deserves."

In the room below she could hear her lady in waiting stirring. Soon, she would bring food; nourishment and sustenance for a royal prince, and after that it would be time to douse the candle and sleep. The routine was as familiar and as lacklustre as the lines on her own hand. She sighed, and spoke again to the silent garden.

"Nineteen children. That is what I bore him; nineteen, and each one healthy and sweet and alive." The screaming ordeals of those births were clear in her mind still; as was the image of her husband's eyes, cold and dead as something resurrected from beneath the earth, as he stared down at her where she lay exhausted from her travail and in a voice of calm reason, called her slut and harlot and fornicator, before turning to the midwife and ordering the newborn infant to be taken away.

The boys, she knew, had been dropped into the old, foetid and long-disused well in the east courtyard, and left to sink or swim. Babies did not swim; or at least, not for long. The girls had received more kindly treatment; their throats were cut, which was quicker and thus an example of the king's mercy. Mercy. Nineteen children. Nineteen sad proclamations that the royal heir had not survived the birth. Sorrow and sympathy and public grief, the king stricken, the queen prostrate... And a swift and discreet series of executions as those who knew and might tattle were dispatched to a better — or more convenient —place, while the few who knew and would not tattle went quietly about their proper business and forgot, with consummate and long practised skill, what they had heard and seen. Until all that remained to show that the queen's children had ever existed were nineteen sculptures in the spiral garden.

And all because of one man's insane mistrust. All because the colour of their hair was *wrong*. For each babe had been as dark as she was. Not one had inherited its father's fine red tresses, and the seeds of suspicion were sown as the king asked himself if they might, just might, be another man's get.

The king, of course, had never believed in his heart, or in whatever icy travesty it was that beat under his ribs, that his wife was unfaithful. Had he done so, then she would have died with her first child. In truth the queen did not know how the seed had taken root, for the beginning of it had been so long ago that memory could not be trusted now. But once begun, it had run away like a horse out of control, until its power over the king was such that it became second nature to him to take no chances. So, the children died and their father grew madder, while their mother kept her tongue and thus her head and submitted to the yearly ritual of birth and death which he forced upon her. Even now, when there could be no doubt, the ritual would be repeated yet again at this child's coming, if the sign the king craved was not there. But it would be there. The queen smiled to herself, remembering the demon's promise. He had promised, too, that she would live long enough to witness her husband's pleasure, and she relished that part of the bargain above all. His face. His smile. His satisfaction and his pride. She would laugh with him, as joyous as he. But he would never know the meaning of her laughter.

A soft scratching at the door announced her lady, who came in bearing a covered tray, her manner subdued as mice and solemn as priests. Time to eat, then time to sleep. The queen smiled at her with more warmth and regard than usual, and when the business of setting out the food was done, the lady went away feeling gratified. A small kindness, the queen thought. The woman did her best, and she would not have to endure the boredom of her mistress's imprisonment for much longer.

She began, daintily, to eat the meal before her, to sustain the health of the child within.

※ ※ ※

The queen was brought to bed in the small hours of the morning of Hunter's-Feast. When the news was announced, the king's physician gave private and profound thanks that Her Grace's timing had proved his own predictions almost to the hour, and went to the Tower of Contemplation with face wreathed in smiles.

The queen was very calm. Natural enough, for the rigours of childbirth were nothing new to her, and the physician carried out an examination and assured himself that all was well before leaving the midwife and her women to the cruder necessities. The king, as always, was waiting in the audience room with his favoured courtiers. He received the physician's report with a nod and no discernible change of expression, gave orders that he was to be informed when the child was delivered, then lapsed into his customary silence, staring out of the window. The physician withdrew. No one spoke. Everyone continued to wait.

The labour continued, with respites, throughout the day – then an hour after sunset the baby was born. The physician took one look at it and went running from the tower and through the corridors to the audience room, almost colliding disastrously with the pikemen on guard as he reached the door. There was a brief scuffle, a breathless exchange of words, and the carved doors were flung open.

"Sire!" The physician stumbled to a breathless halt before the throne, and the courtiers held their own breaths as they saw the king tense and stare.

"What news?" the king demanded. His hand tightened on the throne's arms until his knuckles turned white. "What news?"

The physician's smile stretched from ear to ear. "A boy, Sire! A little prince, healthy and lusty as any child ever born! And ... he has red hair!"

She felt a shadow fall across her, and opened her eyes to see her husband standing at the bedside, gazing down at her and at the baby in her arms. By the candlelight she saw the glitter in his eyes, a gleam of eagerness, half-suppressed as yet but only waiting for his own sight to confirm the truth before it broke free. She counted to nine while he continued to gaze. Then, without turning his head, he addressed the hovering physician.

"Hold the child up. In the light."

The baby made a small, snuffling noise as it was lifted. The king stared at it. At its hair. The baby's mouth opened and closed gummily, as if it was trying to smile or even to laugh, and the index finger of the king's right hand twitched. The queen lay still, observing. Then the king's narrow lips curved. He was not accustomed to smiling, but for one such as him it was a passable effort.

"A son," he said. The smile grew wider. "I have a son." He turned to his wife, and now when he looked at her there was a new light in his eyes, a light of pleasure and, almost, of affection. "Well, madam. I am very gratified. I am very pleased." Then, perhaps remembering belatedly that she, too, had played her part, he added, "And you — you are well enough?"

The queen returned his smile. "Well enough, by your grace, my lord."

"Good. Good." The king studied the baby again, thinking of names and celebrations and nurseries and toys and tutors. His caution over all the preceding years was suddenly vindicated in his mind. It had been no more than caution; an unfortunate but rational necessity, and now fully justified by this happy outcome. His son. *His* son. Crown prince, and heir to a kingdom. At last, he was a contented man.

The physician ventured, "He is as like to Your Grace as could be."

The king grunted tolerantly. "Like enough, I grant you." Then, to the queen, "I will have a gift fashioned for you to mark this occasion. A necklace, I think. Rubies. And a bracelet to wear on your wrist."

The queen said, "Thank you, my lord."

Satisfied, he stepped back from the bed. "Ensure that the queen wants for nothing. We shall celebrate. We shall all celebrate the birth of my son!" He started to turn towards the door – then stopped as something beyond the tower window caught his attention. Outside, a wind had risen. The bushes, turning gold and just a little bare now that autumn had come, were rustling, and by the light of the rising moon and the torches in palace windows the garden was clearly visible. For just one moment it seemed to the king that the stone spirals, the memorials to other and less pleasant times that now could be put away, were gone. In their places, instead, twenty-five small figures gazed up at the window from which the king looked down. They were smiling. And among them, taller and deeply shadowed yet clear to his eyes and shocking him with a stab of recognition, was the shade of his dead first wife.

The king drew in a sharp breath. He blinked; and the figures vanished. There was only the garden and the stones and the bushes stirring under the wind's touch. Illusions. They had been nothing more than illusions and tricks of the night. Or (and the King's composure returned fully at the thought) if there *was* significance in them, then they were surely a sign of good fortune, for they had smiled at him, as though conferring a blessing from beyond the grave. A blessing on him, and on his son.

The physician, who had seen the change in his liege but not the cause of it, ventured uneasily, "Sire... Is something amiss?"

"Amiss?" The king regarded him, though his thoughts were clearly elsewhere. "No. All is well. All is *very* well."

The feasting was over, but wine was still flowing in the banqueting-hall when, at midnight, word was brought to the king that the queen was dead. The king received the news without overt emotion, only nodding slowly and continuing to gaze with obsessive pride at the tiny prince in the wet-nurse's arms. Tears sprang to the nurse's eyes, but a frown from the king stemmed them and she bowed her head over her charge again, settling herself more comfortably on her stool beside the throne. An unexpected relapse, the physician said, wringing his hands nervously, but a peaceful and, he was sure, painless departure from the world. Indeed, just before the moment of death the queen was heard to laugh very softly and gently. The king nodded again. A pity. His wife would not now see the prince grow, which was cause for sadness; but she had, at least, done her duty before death claimed her, and that was consolation. Sad for the prince to lose his mother. A mother was central to a child's wellbeing; it would therefore be advisable for him to marry again before too long...

Aloud, he said, "We shall mourn the queen when the prince's celebration time is over. Until then, there will be no public announcement of her passing." He reached out and touched the baby's face, tickling its chin. The baby beamed and gurgled; the king smiled back with abstracted pleasure, thinking of toys and tutors. "My son," he said. "*My* son."

❈ ❈ ❈

The crown prince is a sturdy boy now, almost twelve years old, and everyone declares that in all respects he is the image of his father. They do not know, and will not know for some years yet, how right they are.

The king has married again; a bride of a similar age to himself and thus too old to bear children, which suits him well and avoids any future problems of rivalry or worse. The prince is very fond of the new queen (as she is still known), and she of him, though sometimes she wonders privately at the uncommonly adult intelligence and insight of her stepson, who is after all still only a child. But then he has the best of everything, including the best of learning, for he will rule one day and must be worthy of his role.

The garden at the foot of the Tower of Contemplation is still diligently tended, and twenty-seven stone spirals now stand among the flower beds. The memorial to the prince's mother is especially elegant; a token, perhaps, of the king's gratitude, or at least appreciation, for her final gift to him. The prince often goes to the garden, and always alone. He sits beside his mother's stone, and he recites to himself the names of all his brothers and sisters, or rather, half-brothers and half-sisters, just as his mother used to do. No one is permitted to disturb him in the garden; though he can be seen from the palace windows, smiling and happy and with the sun glinting warmly on his red hair. So like his father's. And when he has finished his recitation, the prince thinks about his thirteenth birthday, now not long away. At thirteen, he will be officially a man. Able to rule. Able to command. He has already made his plans for the first command he will give; an order to a stonemason, not within the palace but at a town some distance away. A skilled man, a craftsman, a consummate artist. The prince intends to commission a new spiral, one fit to commemorate a king. A king who will shortly discover the truth about his heir; and who will die of the discovery, in a slow, savage tidal wave of pain and terror. It is of no moment to the prince, but a promise is a promise, and he is, truly, his father's son. Another soul for the reaping. And when the screaming is over, nineteen children and their grieving mother will be waiting to welcome their fallen lord to a new kind of existence that will never, ever end.

 The prince walks in the spiral garden. He thinks his thoughts and he makes his plans; plans, too, for the kingdom that will soon be his to enjoy as he pleases. In many ways he is still a child, so it will amuse him to play, for a while, with this new and special toy. But he will grow up eventually, and when he does, the real enjoyment will begin.

 Though whether the mortals of his court, and of his kingdom, and one day, possibly, of his world, will share the pleasure of their overlord, is a matter that is best, perhaps, not dwelt upon by prudent minds.

HIS TRUE AND ONLY WIFE

Years ago, when they were both children, Leah had said, "I'll marry you one day. When we're grown and Mammati is dead. She'll have to die sometime, and then I'll be your true and only wife."

Carolan had only smiled in the slow, pleasing way he had and pulled another grass stem to strip and chew, savouring the sweet-sharp taste while he enjoyed the spring sun's warmth on his back. It was just another of Leah's promises, another of the wild and secret ambitions they so often talked of down here by the old well in the valley where no one ever came to disturb their games and fantasies. In truth, he probably would marry her one day. It would be the natural thing to do, after all, for weren't they the oldest of friends and the oldest of cohorts? And her mother would die. One day. One far-off, happy day the old witch would meet her just end. Carolan hastily crossed himself for such an unholy and unworthy thought, but it was true nonetheless. One day, Leah would be free.

But to the disappointment not only of Carolan and Leah but of the whole village, the old woman lived on far beyond the span that natural justice should have dictated. Leah continued to suffer under her dictatorial and increasingly eccentric rule, and the bruises and black eyes that had been a part of her life since she had first learned to walk still blossomed on her like flowers on a bush. And as Mammati grew older and madder her daughter also suffered under the stigma of being increasingly ostracised by their neighbours.

No one held Leah to blame, of course. A child has no say in its own parentage, and it wasn't her fault that she was a bastard get and her mother one of the devil's own; indeed, twice a year, on Forgiveness Day and Sinners' Night, Father Borlagh exhorted his flock to say solemn prayers for Leah's salvation. Yet though they obeyed their priest with a good will, the villagers were less generous when it came to welcoming the child herself in their midst. Hapless victim of circumstance she might be, but that didn't make her any less the witch's daughter. And by the time she was nine years old a few of the tabbies were already hinting at the growing and unmistakable physical likeness she bore to her Mammati.

The gossip of the tabbies was lost on Carolan, who, like any wise boy, had better things to do than keep company with old women. Leah was his special friend, and one day he would probably marry her. That was all he knew and all he cared to know; the future with its adult complications could look after itself for a few years yet. However, Carolan's grandmother, whose sharp eyes missed very little in the village, had begun to whisper certain observations in his mother's ear about her son and That Girl. And his mother, alarmed by what she heard, joined forces with the old dame to nag her husband into taking action. Carolan's father was by nature a placid and uncomplicated man, and in his heart he wanted no truck with their speculations. Carolan was an unfledged puppy still learning his letters at dame school; what did he know or care about girls as anything but playmates? But the women persisted, each argument grew shriller and angrier, and at last Carolan's father capitulated. Something must be done, they constantly told him. Very well, something *would* be done, as it seemed it was the only way to make them cease their pestering and allow him to live his life in peace.

So on his eleventh birthday Carolan was apprenticed to Laery the carter. The news caused a stir in the village; Laery was a highly-respected man in a highly-respected profession – a man of the world, too, for rumour had it that he had on occasion travelled as much as twenty miles from his home village in the course of his work. A private man and a lifelong bachelor, he had never taken an apprentice before, though many young hopefuls had tried to ingratiate themselves under his dour eye. How Carolan's father had persuaded him to break with his habit no one knew, but it was commonly believed that the miracle must have been helped upon its way by a healthy contribution from the family's purse. Still, that only proved Carolan Senior to be a wiser man than he looked, for with no natural heir to follow in Laery's footsteps his apprentice would surely inherit the prosperous business when Laery was finally called to his maker. Young Carolan, they said, was a lucky little devil. And the tabbies, nodding sagely and sliding their gazes aside in an eloquently expressive way that bypassed any need for words, implied that his family was lucky in more ways than one, for with their boy gone to Laery's village the question of That Girl would soon be a burden lifted from their shoulders.

The blacksmith's wife happened to meet Leah at the well in the valley when Leah went to fetch water for her mother, and gleefully told her the news. Leah received the information in stony silence, then walked away into the wood and waited for the smirking woman to depart. When she had gone and Leah was sure she was out of earshot, she returned to the well and screamed down into its stale depths with all the strength her lungs possessed. The scream echoed back as though a devil's imp was crouching down there in the water and mocking her, and when Leah finally realised that this was no comfort, no ease to the pain inside her, she straightened and stared for a very long time at the rustling trees that climbed the valley slope. What she thought was private; what she felt would never be uttered to another living soul. But she was resolved in what she must do. Carolan was gone; but one day he would come back to her. By then, she told herself fiercely, by then it would be different. And, hating Mammati to the depths of her soul, she turned away from the well and trudged back towards the lonely, cramped and loathsome cottage that she must for a while yet call home.

❈ ❈ ❈

On the spring morning when she came back from an early foray to market and found Mammati stiff and cold in her bed, Leah knelt down by the hearthstone and offered a prayer of thanksgiving. Then, soberly and diligently, she set about the necessary tasks. Father Borlagh wouldn't consider for one moment the idea of burying Mammati on hallowed ground, and so a wake, such as might have been held for anyone else in the district, was clearly out of the question. So Leah lit a candle and sat silently by her mother's corpse until sunset. Then she left the house, took a shovel and walked to the end of the vegetable patch, where she dug a hole, sternly resisting the temptation to sing as she worked. Heaving the old woman out of bed and along the overgrown path almost defeated her, but she struggled on until at last she reached her goal, then had the satisfaction of seeing the withered old face for the last time before the first spadeful of earth thumped into the hole with a soft and faintly obscene sound, and covered Mammati's features for ever. Silently, methodically, Leah replaced the soil she had dug and patted down the resulting shallow mound. Then she set the shovel aside, put the palms of her hands together and said, "Day behind me, night before me, bless the mother who once bore me, God help us all, amen," in a flatly dutiful monotone. That done, she stared at the mound for a few minutes, still not entirely convinced that the earth wouldn't suddenly fountain into the air, and Mammati burst out of her grave screeching with laughter at the joke she had played on her daughter. But nothing happened. Only an owl called somewhere in the wood, and Leah knew that owls were harbingers of death. All was well, then. She was truly free at last.

    She walked back to the house. The hearth fire had gone out, but that didn't matter; she had bought more oil for the lamps this morning. She picked up the tin in which the oil was kept, and spilled its contents all over the floor. The familiar, fishy smell made her nostrils curl but she smiled at the stench, for this was the last, the very last time that she would be forced to endure it. Then she took Mammati's tinderbox, retreated to the doorway and lit a scrap of rag. It caught, the flame licking bright and clean and quick as though the elements themselves favoured her tonight. Leah's smile widened; she tossed the rag onto the oil-soaked floor, and as the first *whoof* of yellow fire erupted through the room she turned and ran, leaping and dancing through the vegetable patch and over Mammati's grave and away into the woods, with Carolan's name on her lips.

❖ ❖ ❖

"Young Carolan?" said the wheelwright's wife, smiling unpleasantly in the way that Leah had come to know well over the years. "No. Haven't seen hide nor hair of him for months gone by." She sounded pleased by her inability to help. Leah, who had spent the night dancing for sheer glee in the woods and had walked into the village with the coming of morning, tossed her unbound auburn curls so that they glinted in the sunlight – she saw the envious flash in the woman's eyes – and strode away.

"Carolan?" The blacksmith (his wife, thankfully, wasn't in the yard this morning) shook his head gravely. "No, lass, we've seen nothing of him here, nor his master Laery neither. You'd best inquire at his father's cottage."

At the cottage she was confronted by the old dame, a crone now with two blackthorn sticks to support her and a temper soured with the rigours of time. "My grandson," she told Leah, "is away in Laery's village as he's been for ten years past, and his Mamaw and Dadaw are away there too now, to see him wed."

Leah stood very still. "Wed...?"

"Wed." The crone repeated the word emphatically and with satisfaction. "So there's nothing here for you, miss. Away with you; away, and don't show your trollop's face on my threshold a second time." And she shut the door in Leah's face.

For a long time Leah stood outside the gate, staring at the cottage, which seemed to stare belligerently back, and telling herself over and again that it was not, it was not, it was *not* true. It was *not*. Wasn't she to be Carolan's only wife? Hadn't they promised? It was *not true*.

An odd, broken little sound came from her throat at last, and she turned and ran, her feet thudding in the dust, away to the priest's house.

She had never dared to approach this place before. Mammati had forbidden it, and even if she'd been prepared to risk defying Mammati there was always the shadow of the church behind the house to deter her, every stone seeming to frown down a silent anathema. But now she didn't think of Mammati or anathemas or anything else; she stumbled through the gate and up the hard-trodden path, and hammered with her fists on the forbidding oak door.

Father Borlagh was at home, and opened the door to her savage knocking. He stared at the wild-eyed, wild-haired witch's daughter, and his eyebrows, like small, prickly hedgehogs above the button-black eyes, came sharply together in a frown.

"Leah? What is it, girl? What do you want?"

Leah glared back at him, defiance and defence and determination radiating from every pore of her. "Mammati's dead," she said. "I did the right thing by her. I sat by her all day yesterday and then I buried her in the garden and I said God-Help-Us over her, and now I've come to find Carolan."

"Ah." Father Borlagh, like all good priests of his persuasion, knew enough about his flock and their doings to comprehend her meaning immediately. "Carolan, is it? Well, now..."

"I saw *her*," Leah interjected before he could continue. "The old beldame, his gammer. She said Carolan's to be wed!"

Father Borlagh didn't have to answer; his expression gave the truth away immediately, and to Leah the mingling of embarrassment, shame and irritation that flowered across his plump face was more terrible than if he had pronounced a curse on her there and then. She felt something dear and precious shrivelling up inside her, withering her heart like a dead leaf, and she stared at the priest, willing his features to change again, willing him to laugh suddenly and pat her head as he sometimes used to when she was little and he couldn't avoid meeting her in the street, and tell her that the beldame was joking and it was not, *was not* true.

Her prayers went unanswered. Father Borlagh began to nod slowly, and seemed to go on nodding for a very long time. At last Leah couldn't bear the silence any longer, and she burst out, "When?"

The priest stopped nodding and the tip of his tongue appeared, wetting his lower lip. "Now then; what's the day to be? Not that I'd be sure to know of course, seeing that the family didn't see fit even to invite their own priest to the nuptials, let alone ask me to perform the holy rite, and if that's not a sign of the heathen times we live in then I don't know what is…"

With a silent ferocity that owed more than a nod to Mammati, Leah wished a plague of warts on the old fool and an imp to bite of his blethering tongue. *"When?"* she screeched.

"Today, I think it is." Abruptly his eyes grew hard, like little chips "Yes. Today. In Laery's village."

Leah's heart began to pound under her ribs, hurting her, squashing the breath from her lungs. What was the hour? How much time did she have? Her voice sawing in her throat as if from desperate want of water, she said, "How far is it? Laery's village – how far, and which way?"

The priest frowned. "Now, child, that's not a wise thing to think of! Calla's a fine and good and handsome girl, and she'll be the right wife for Carolan. You mustn't—"

"*I'm* the right wife for Carolan!" *Calla*, she thought, and stored the name away securely in her mind. Mammati would have known what to do about Calla.

"Now, Leah!" Father Borlagh drew himself up to his full height, so that the wind caught his black robe and made it flap like demon's wings. "That is enough! Will you try to ruin Carolan's wedding, which should be the happiest day of his life?"

She clenched her teeth and spat through them, "I love him!"

"Indeed you don't, or you'd have the good sense to let him go to a woman who's a fit match for his station in life!" Father Borlagh rejoined tartly. "Carolan is a young man of substance now, with a fine future before him."

Leah started to shake. "I'm not good enough for him? Is that what you're saying to me?"

"Well, if you'll insist on forcing it from my own lips – yes. That is what I'm saying to you." His face took on a pious look now. "I'll not speak ill of the departed, so I've nothing to say about the black soul of your late mother. But she *was* your mother whether or not you chose her, and a witch's daughter brought up like a savage in the woods and without the sanctity of baptism and righteous fear of her betters is *not* the wife for a goodly young man like Carolan!"

In the hateful years under Mammati's yoke Leah had learned above all else to control her naturally hectic temper, and she controlled it now – at least outwardly. Her head drooped, her feet scuffed at the hard-packed earth beneath them, and Father Borlagh did not know her well enough to recognise the difference between true capitulation and a reasonably skilled acting performance.

She said, in the voice of one who had reluctantly accepted defeat, "How far is Laery's village, Father?"

"Well now, I don't think I should tell you that." But his tone had softened; even if she was past saving he would be a hard man and a poor priest if he couldn't find it in himself to pity her just a little. "Why would you want to wear out your feet to no good purpose? Carolan's gone from you now, child. Be content, and trust in God to make you a better girl."

"Yes," Leah said, nodding and taking care that he couldn't see her expression. "Yes, Father, you're right, and I will. But I'd like to see Carolan one last time. To wish him good fortune."

The man was a fool, she thought. Either that, or so vain that he couldn't countenance the idea that she might not have heeded his words of wisdom. His voice softened still further – it sounded how a dead thing smelled in the summer, sweet and sickly, with something rotten at its core – and he reached out as though to lay a hand on her shoulder, then thought better of it. "Well now, Leah, that would be the right and noble thing to do, and so perhaps I'll tell you after all if you're so set on it. Laery's village lies half a day's walk to the southeast, and you'll know Laery's house by the sign of the horse and wagon that hangs over the lintel."

"Southeast. The sign of the horse and wagon." She looked up and smiled so guilelessly that Father Borlagh wondered for a rash moment if she might not have been her Mammati's child at all but a foundling. "Thank you, Father."

"You'll thank me best by being a good girl now that the witch has gone." He signed a blessing at her. "I'll say a prayer for you before my own altar."

"Say another one for Carolan's new wife, Father." The nature of Leah's smile changed subtly, then suddenly the one cracked bell in the church tower began to bang out a summons, calling the good people of the village to morning devotions. Over the noise Leah shouted, "She'll be the one who needs it!"

Father Borlagh watched her run away down the street, then

56

turned and, like a great black bat, swooped towards the church to greet his flock, wondering just what it was that the girl had said.

❦ ❦ ❦

Leah tricked a passing farmer into giving her a ride on his cart by showing him her legs and promising him favours as soon as they reached a quiet enough spot. She sat atop the cabbage-sacks for two-thirds of the distance to Laery's village before the man finally insisted on payment, at which she sprang down and sprinted away with his furious curses following her along the road. The sun had passed the zenith by then and, aware that time was not her friend, she settled into a taxing but necessary jog until at last a sizeable village came into view ahead. As she limped past the boundary stone, she heard the bells of a finer church than Father Borlagh's begin to ring out a celebration peal.

Leah stopped in the middle of the deserted street, which suddenly seemed to her like a scene from some desolate hell. She was too late. The white cords and the red cords had been tied, the shoes had been filled with grain, and the bells were announcing the holy union of Carolan and Calla.

She reached the church in time to see the bridal party emerge. Though she hadn't set eyes on him for ten years she would have known Carolan instantly even without the scarlet bridegroom's clothes to mark him, for though he was so much taller and his chest and shoulders so much broader and his hair now cut short at the sides and long at the back in the fashion of the well-to-do market towns, the eyes and the smile were those of the Carolan she had loved for all of her life. Beside him, in a white gown, her black hair bound up with twining ivy, and the bride's bouquet of yellow and red in her hand, Calla walked in the place that should have been Leah's. She was lovely. No, Leah amended with a surge of spitefulness; not lovely, for her eyebrows were too heavy, her mouth too generous and her body too sturdy for real beauty. But handsome. Even in the depths of her bitterness Leah couldn't deny that Carolan's new wife was handsome.

From behind a moss-grown gravestone that, had she been able to read, would have told her that beneath this earth lay the blessed remains of Tomas, son of Ruar and Maeve, departed this world aged seven months and now sleeping in the arms of angels, Leah watched the procession leave for the churchyard. Carolan's and Calla's hands were tied together by the holy cords, and to the strains of a fife and tabor the wedding guests laughed and shouted and threw petals and wheat grains over the couple. A Fool in motley pranced in and out of the group, whinnying like a horse, and Leah's lip curled in a sneer for she knew how much these professional luck-bringers charged for their services. If Carolan had married his true wife he'd have had no cause to hire a Fool to ensure good fortune. Now, though... she smiled. He and his handsome girl would need more than a prancing, posturing charlatan to stand between them and what their futures would hold.

The party was moving on, the sounds of rejoicing growing fainter as the wedding guests turned out of the churchyard and away along the street. Leah didn't attempt to follow them. She knew how to find Laery's house when she needed to, and until then she was content to bide her time. She sat down behind the gravestone, and idly began to pick daisies to weave into a chain to wear around her neck.

❁ ❁ ❁

The bell-tower clock was striking midnight when the first wedding guests began to leave. Laery's house still shook to the sounds of drum and fiddle and the stamping of feet; the hardiest would stay on dancing and drinking long into the night, but gradually the number of celebrants was beginning to thin out.

Carolan, as befitted the bridegroom, personally saw each party away. He was returning to the house after the third such farewell when a shadow moved in the hedge beside the gate and a figure stepped into his path. She said, "Carolan," and he didn't recognise her voice. Then, in a reflection of light from inside the house, he saw the colour of her eyes and the guinea gold glint of her hair. Ten years fell away, and he remembered the girl who had been his playmate and confidante at the well in the valley so long ago.

"Leah..." Astonishment filled his voice – and something else. Chagrin? Guilt? Leah wasn't sure. "What are *you* doing here?"

She continued to look him squarely in the face and he thought she smiled, though the dark made it hard to tell.

"I came to find you," she said. Her voice was different, older, as it must be, of course, though he found it disconcerting – and with an edge to it that hadn't been there in the old days. "Mammati's dead, so I came to remind you of our promise."

"Promise?" Carolan was baffled. "What promise was that, Leah?"

She drew breath with a sharp hiss, like a cat. "That I'd be your true and only wife." A pause. "You've forgotten, haven't you? You've forgotten what we said!"

"Of course I've not forgotten!"

But she knew from his tone that he was lying, and she fired back at him. "You *have* forgotten! You were eight years old and I was seven, and we said—"

"*Eight?*" Suddenly there was laughter and relief in his voice. "By all the angels, Leah, we were nothing more than babbies! We must have said a hundred crazy things to each other in those days, a thousand, a million! If we were to keep to all our babbies' promises we'd be in a pretty scrape by now!"

In the darkness Leah's teeth showed white. "That wasn't a babbies' promise, and you know it wasn't! We pledged ourselves, Carolan, you for my true and only husband and me for your true and only wife! And now—" She swung round, one arm indicating Laery's house and the noisy festivities. "Now you've forsaken all that we said and you've married *her*. Why, Carolan? *Why?*"

"Leah, it was just a game between us! We're grown now, we're different."

"I'm not different. I still love you. And I know you still love me. Deep down, you do."

Carolan hesitated, then decided that he must say it. If he didn't tell her the truth now, coldly and bluntly, she would cling to her fancy and he wouldn't be rid of her. Better to earn her hatred than have her following him about like a dog and upsetting Calla. He said, "I don't love you, Leah. I love my wife, my Calla. That's why I married her and not you."

"That's not true! You *do* love me!"

"I do not. Look into my face and I'll say it again. I do not love you, Leah, and I don't want you interfering in my new life and trying to spoil it. Whatever we might or might not have said in the past, we're grown up now and things are different. I don't wish you any ill, Leah, and I'm glad for you that your Mammati finally died and let you free. But I don't want to see you any more. I want you to go away."

Leah froze for a few moments. Then, with a new eagerness in her voice, she said, "Let *us* go away, Carolan! Together – let's go tonight, now, and then you can forget all this and come back to me, and—"

"Holy blood and bones, haven't you listened to a word I've said?" Carolan interrupted incredulously. "No, Leah, *no!* I don't want you, I don't want to be with you." He paused. "And if you don't go away now, this minute, I shall tell the priest and he'll come and *drive* you away! Do you understand me now?"

She did. She stepped back, feeling the wild hope crumbling to grave-dust within her. "All right," she said in a new, gentler tone. "I'll go, if that's what you think you want. But you're telling lies to your own self, Carolan. I know that, and before long you'll know it too." Then she smiled, and with her face in deepest shadow the smile took on dire meaning. "Enjoy your time with your handsome new wife while you can, for it won't last. I'll see to that, Carolan. I'll see to that!"

And, brushing past him with a flick of hair and a whirl of dusty skirt, she ran away down the dark street like a fleeing ghost.

❈ ❈ ❈

Six months later, Carolan and his wife came home to his own village. The idea was Laery's; the carter was an ambitious man and considered that his apprentice had learned enough to be entrusted with the running of a second branch of the business. With horses and wagons established in two villages at once, Laery's trade could expand in the grand manner. Laery would prosper; he would be wealthy; he would become a *personage*.

There was also the matter of what was best for Calla. To the great disappointment of everyone from the priests to Carolan's gammer, Calla had so far failed to get with child. Neither fervent prayers nor gifts to the church had solved the problem, and even a God-Help-Us, said before the altar with special dispensation from the Grand Manse, achieved nothing. At last Father Dorrit, who ruled over Laery's village and had married the young couple in the first place, had taken Calla aside and, after close questioning and a stern lecture about her holy duty, declared that the reason for her failure was perfectly obvious to anyone who had the brains they were born with. How could a lone woman in a household of menfolk be expected to keep her mind on womanly matters? In order to learn and prosper as she should, Calla needed to be among other women. And with her own mother dead then the only decent place for her was under the roof of Carolan's mamaw and gammer, who could instruct her in the obligations proper to a young wife.

In some ways Laery was sad to see the couple go. Since Calla's arrival his house had never been cleaner nor his meals more appetising. But he saw the virtues of a good business opportunity, and besides, he wasn't in the habit of arguing with Father Dorrit. So with Laery's blessing, and driving Laery's new cart with which he was to establish his trade, Carolan brought his bride home.

The village decided to hold a welcoming party. It was the gammer's notion, and she enlisted Father Borlagh's help in the organising, hobbling determinedly on her blackthorn sticks to the priest's house. At first Father Borlagh wasn't inclined to co-operate; he was still harbouring indignation at being excluded from the nuptials three months ago and felt that to be asked to pronounce a belated blessing on the marriage was adding insult to injury. But the gammer wore him down and at last he gave way; so on the day of Harvest Feast the cracked bell in the stern old tower clanged its summons, and a cheerful procession wound its way along the path and into the church's embrace to see Carolan and Calla kneel together before Father Borlagh.

No one, least of all Carolan, gave a thought to Leah that day. In fact no one had given a thought to Leah for the best part of three months now. For a while after her Mammati's death it had been different. People – and the womenfolk in particular – were curious to know how she would fare and what she would do, and on one historic day she had even ventured into the church during Sin-Forgiveness, sitting alone at the back and listening to the singing and the sermons. Father Borlagh had entertained brief hopes that Leah might at last be persuaded to see the light, but then he reasoned that, being her mother's daughter and a shameless, disobedient and unruly creature by nature, she was more likely to be bent on mischief than on devotion. So when the service was over he withheld the words of encouragement he might otherwise have offered, and swept past her without so much as a glance.

Leah didn't come to church again but she was still seen about the village, usually on market days when she came to buy food. No one knew where she got her money, though speculation was rife; some said her Mammati had left a long purse, some said Leah went robbing innocent households at night, while the great majority of the women agreed that Payment For Certain Favours must be easy enough for such a trollop to come by and that Leah was a disgrace and should be driven away.

However, Leah stayed, and as time went by and she caused no trouble the villagers learned to tolerate her. Curiosity began to wane; though there was a brief flurry of renewed interest when a small deputation went out one day to the house in the woods, to see for themselves how the girl was living. They found only a patch of blackened ground where the house had stood, and Leah had obviously moved herself elsewhere. Intrigued, but not sufficiently to trouble to search for her, the visitors filled their hats and aprons with ripe but neglected vegetables from the overrun garden — for didn't the angels themselves weep at the sight of good food going to waste? — and went home.

Leah knew of the callers. She had seen them from her vantage point high in a nearby tree, and had watched as they poked about and muttered and chattered. She didn't care that they had taken the vegetables; indeed, she was greatly amused by the thought that the village would feed blithely tonight on crops which, in their turn, had been fed by Mammati's corrupting corpse. She didn't need the food, for the woods provided plenty for anyone who knew where and how to look for it, and she had found enough coin under Mammati's bed to buy whatever the woods didn't provide. She did not need the villagers, either. She knew what they said about her when she strode in among them on market days, tossing her brazen hair defiantly while the womenfolk stared and whispered. And that was funny too, for it couldn't have been further from the truth. Leah could have earned money: she was pretty enough and wise enough. But she had other ideas. She was saving herself for one man, as she always had done, as she always would do. And when she heard that Carolan and his wife were returning to the district she danced a silent, triumphant dance alone under the moon, and returned to her crude shelter in an old, hollow oak tree, to make her plans.

❖ ❖ ❖

So, when the procession went into the church for the blessing to be pronounced, Leah was ready. She had learned of the blessing, and the party that was to follow, through snatches of gossip overheard on market day, and she had secretly watched the tables being set out in the lane before Carolan's father's house to accommodate the flood of celebrants who would return from the church at noon. Now, emerging from concealment, she squinted at the sky and the climbing sun in a way that, had she only known it, was quite startlingly reminiscent of her Mammati. An hour or more to go. The village was deserted. She had plenty of time.

    Leah moved from her hiding place with all the nonchalance of a cat about to steal meat from the master's table with master none the wiser. And there was death in her heart and mayhem in her mind as she approached the first and largest table...

❖ ❖ ❖

First, there was to be feasting. Then, when no man, woman or child could accommodate another single mouthful of meat or bread or cake or blackberry pie, there would be dancing; a riot of jigs, reels and strip-the-willows to shake down the food and make room for more. The solemn business of the day was over and done with, and even Father Borlagh, mellow with the beer and cider that flowed as copiously as water from the valley well, had unbuttoned the top three inches of his stiff vestments and was cracking jokes with the best of them.

Before the dancing began, though, there was one more formality to be observed. Carolan was no longer the callow boy who had left home to begin his apprenticeship. He was a man now in his own right; a man of place, a man of substance. So it was only proper and fitting that he should lead the merry company in the traditional toast to good health, long life and the good guidance of God and his angels to make blessed saints of all present when their time came. Dutifully and gladly Carolan rose from his seat, and his arm linked with the arm of his beloved wife, Calla, and in a gesture of mutual devotion they drank deeply from each other's cups; the special cups that had been set aside, ready filled, to await this moment.

And Carolan, the light and the joy and the love of Leah's life and existence, drank the poison that the dark, secret forest had yielded. The poison that Leah had distilled and created to make a widower of him, and to free him to be, as he must, her true and only husband.

❈ ❈ ❈

She could do nothing. They carried him first into his father's house, and when the women declared that he was beyond their help they carried him to the church, where Father Borlagh absolved him of all his sins and commended him to his maker, though Carolan was no longer able to hear or see or know anything of the words that were said or the tears that were wept over his motionless, glassy-eyed body. And when at last it was over, and the stunned and helplessly shuddering widow was borne in the embrace of two strong men through the leather-studded door and down the path and under the frowning, indifferent gaze of the lych-gate, which had seen so many of the dead, and so many of the bereaved, in its long and silent life, Leah crouched behind a headstone, curled like an aborted foetus that had never known a life independent of the womb. She was beyond weeping. The tears were there, but they were beyond her ability to shed. She was dust. Blood and flesh and bones; all dust. Sere soil where not one green shoot could grow. Horror and guilt, twin monsters, inseparable demons before which Father Borlagh himself would have thrown down the sword of righteousness and bowed his grizzled head, had their claws in her soul; and Leah was lost.

For Leah, who had loved Carolan with all the passion and jealousy and possessiveness of her yearning, twisted, fearsome heart, was mad. A quiet and strange and almost peaceful madness. It was in her eyes; it glowed from them as though they truly were the windows of her soul.

And those windows on her soul, to a dispassionate observer, might have suggested that she wasn't done with Carolan yet.

❋ ❋ ❋

They buried him near the yew tree in the southwesterly side of the graveyard; a position, Father Borlagh said, that a man could rightly be proud of. The whole village turned out for the wake and the interment that followed, and Laery came on his other cart, with Father Dorrit sitting beside him. At the graveside they all wept and said God-Help-Us and laid purple flowers on the newly turned soil, and they ignored the mason's spelling mistakes as they admired the headstone, and they ignored the bristling between Father Borlagh and Father Dorrit, and when the last spadeful of earth was filled in and tamped down they put their hats back on their heads and returned to Carolan's father's house for the drinking to begin in earnest.

Calla, they said, was bearing up well, all things considered. To be sure, she hadn't spoken a word all day and her face was as deathly white as the face of poor Carolan in his coffin and her eyes looking like black holes burned into paper; but she was handing round the ale and the mead now, and nodding her solemn thanks at the condolences. A pity, the older women said, that Carolan hadn't managed to get a child on her before he went to the angels, for a child was a great comfort to a woman in widowhood. But then on the other hand perhaps it wasn't such a bad thing, for – and the good God forgive them with her man still warm in his grave, but it was true nonetheless – Calla was young and pretty. Without babbies clinging round her skirts she might yet have the chance for another husband, and good luck to her if she did.

Calla heard all they said, for in the confines of the small room it was impossible not to hear. She said nothing, as was her way. But when dusk came at last, and the gaffers and gammers began to nod and snore while the women crooned to their fractious children and the men, drunk enough now to forget the sad dignity of the occasion, were comfortable before the fire and talking of horses and dogs and gambling, she quietly slipped out of the house by the back way. The moon was up, a chilly, waning crescent in the sky, and it made a ghost of Calla with her black hair and black widow's weeds as she passed through the rickety, creaking gate and on with the slow, dragging footsteps of a soul in anguish towards the church. They were kind, Carolan's people. They were doing their best for her. Even Father Borlagh had patted her hand in an awkward but well meant way, a tear glittering in his eye as he tried to give her comfort. But Calla didn't want comfort. Maybe another day, far in the future, she would be glad of it. Now though, she chose to be with Carolan. She would sit beside him through the lonely night, and sing to him as she used to do in happier times. And even if he couldn't hear her songs, the singing of them might ease her hurt just a little.

In the house another cask of ale had been broached, and the blacksmith's wife had prodded her husband in the ribs and told him to fetch out his fiddle, which he did with a sigh of resignation. The gaffers and gammers woke up at the first strains of music, and the company wavered their way through *Righteous Angels* and *Teach Us The Meaning Of Misery*; two hymns which Father Borlagh considered suitable to the occasion and in which his powerful baritone voice led them. Then, with the formalities observed, the mood changed, and the blacksmith (who was into the spirit of the thing by now) tuned up for 'All Among The Apples', which everyone knew and could roar out with gusto. A few of the more sober souls looked surreptitiously around for Calla but, not finding her, crossed themselves for forgiveness and prepared to bellow along with the best.

Then, as the fiddle played the first lively notes, a shriek from the deepest depths of hell split the night apart.

"Good God and all the saints and angels!" Father Borlagh leaped to his feet. "What in the name of a thousand yammering devils was *that?*"

He and Father Dorrit reached the door together, and there was a moment's confusion as both tried to shoulder the other out of the way and get through first. The door burst open, cool night air sucking heat and smoke and fumes out of the house like a blast from a furnace, and the two priests and the men who now crowded behind them fell back with yells of horror at the sight of a ghastly, spectral figure running at them out of the moonlight, arms flailing, mouth open, and screaming like the legions of the damned.

"*Demons!*" the apparition screeched. "*Red demons! Red demons! At his grave! At his GRA-A-A-AVE!*"

As the men leaped backwards Calla flung herself through the door and sprawled full-length on the rush matting, still flailing, still screaming. It took the blacksmith's wife and three other women to pin her thrashing limbs to the floor, and Father Dorrit hastily recited a Deliverance over her while Carolan's grandmother forced five drops of a nostrum she always carried in her sleeve between the girl's chattering teeth. They calmed Calla's body at last, but her mind was still in the grip of terror and all she would say, over and over again, was, "Red demons at his grave... red demons at his grave..."

There was, said Father Borlagh, only one thing to do. Were they not all God-fearing men and women, and with two priests of God's own company to lead them? Were they not all warriors on the side of the angels? Take up arms, said Father Borlagh, and we shall march to the graveyard and put the forces of evil to such a rout as hasn't been seen since the saints trounced the devils and condemned them to the outer dark!

There were uneasy mutterings at this brave rhetoric, but when Father Dorrit added his considerable voice to that of his rival it was enough to cow them into submission. Better the wrath of demons than the wrath of two of God's own priests. So they took up whatever weapons they could find, from walking-sticks to pots and pans and rolling-pins and good, stout pewter tankards; and, leaving the gammers and the children to comfort Calla as best they could, a righteous army more than thirty strong marched out into the dark to confront the unholy invader.

At the churchyard, moon-shadows reached out long, thin fingers to embrace them. Father Borlagh and Father Dorrit sang another hymn and the army pressed on, through the lych-gate, past the tower stark against the silent sky, under the frowning gaze of the yew tree, which rustled and whispered at them as though murmuring some dire secret.

There were no red demons at Carolan's grave. But the purple flowers were scattered like drops of blood, and the earth which the sexton had tamped so smoothly down had been disturbed, as though something had been digging there with clawed hands, striving to reach what lay below. And the headstone had been uprooted and left to lie like a loaf of mouldering, unleavened bread under the moon's indifferent stare.

Half a mile away, where the woods began their silent encroachment on the village, Leah knelt among the leafmould, hidden by the low-hanging branches of the trees. She stared fixedly, unseeingly towards the village, and the nails of her fingers where they gripped her upper arms were caked black with newly turned soil. Every now and then a great spasm shook her, a palsy of grief and rage that knew no limit and no end. She had *failed*. That creature, that false, usurping hoyden who called herself wife to Carolan, had *dared* to interfere, and Carolan still lay beyond Leah's reach. But she would have him. Leah swore it by God and saints and angels, by demons and unholy serpents, and by the mocking ghost of her own dead Mammati who had taught her the ways of the dark. Next time, she would not fail. Next time she would have her love, her man, her true and rightful husband, in her arms again. And when she did, *nothing* would take him from her.

❈ ❈ ❈

It was all done in the right and proper way. Father Borlagh was man enough to submerge his lingering resentments, and the next day he and Father Dorrit performed a ceremony of exorcism and protection over the restored grave of Carolan. The sun didn't choose to show its face and the observances were conducted amid a dreary, soaking drizzle; but when all was done the two priests repaired to the house of Carolan's father and were well fed, so there was little cause for complaint.

Calla still lay as she had lain since last night, in the top room that was to have housed her marital bed, with Carolan's mother and grandmother constantly in attendance. She was awake and aware of her surroundings, but still all she would say was, "Red demons... red demons..." The beldame declared that this was only to be expected. For hadn't the poor widowed child seen enough to unhinge the most devout soul? Something must be done, she said. Something must be done, or the vile monster would come back as surely as night followed day. Timidly, Carolan's mother suggested that Father Borlagh and Father Dorrit were surely doing all that could be expected; more, indeed, for their cloth granted them solemn powers that were denied to lesser men. But the beldame, with a sniff and a meaningful glare in the direction of the churchyard, replied that priests and prayers and powers were all very well when it was an exorcism you wanted, or a laying on of hands. But when it came to deeds it was quite another matter. Deeds were the domain of women, and it was the women who would act now. They would watch, she said. Turn and turn about, by night and by day, at the place where poor Carolan had been laid to sleep in the arms of his holy maker. And when It returned, as It was certain to do, they would be ready.

Even in her distraught state, Carolan's mother couldn't fail to notice that where poor Calla had cried *They* in the plural, the beldame said *It* in the singular. But she made no comment, for she had learned the beldame's ways long ago and would no more argue with her than with an angel bearing a fiery sword.

The other women, it transpired, were also disinclined to argue with the beldame. They didn't like what she proposed, but in the face of her fierce determination they held their tongues and asked no more questions than Carolan's mother had done. Fathers Borlagh and Dorrit raised no objections either, and one or two uncharitable souls suggested that they were only too glad to have the matter taken out of their hands.

So when darkness fell that night, nine women set out in grim and silent anticipation for the churchyard, with the beldame hobbling in the lead. The sky was clear and the moon riding high and cool above, her arc a light to guide them on their way. One by one, or two by two for the less courageous, they ranged themselves about the graveyard, each with a clear, star-glimmering view of the headstone restored to its place now above the spot where Carolan lay.

And as the midnight hour passed and the moon reached her zenith and thus the height of her power, the beldame's prayers were answered and Calla's red demon returned.

She was singing a song as she came, softly and under her breath but audible nonetheless. As if that wasn't sacrilege enough, she was also swinging a long-handled garden spade, slicing at the tops of churchyard flowers with the newly sharpened blade as she walked.

The spade had seen sterling service over the years. It had dug trenches for vegetables, larger holes for currant bushes and apple trees, and, latterly, a greater hole still for the corpse of Mammati. Now though, Leah had a new purpose in mind for it. Now, it would be the instrument by which she would be reunited with her love, her man, her true and only husband.

Leah was quite, quite mad. But it was a pleasant madness now, for the rage had gone, and the guilt had faded, and the grief... well, the grief would not last. After tonight there would be cause for rejoicing instead, for she and Carolan would be one at last. Leah smiled as she sang, and she skipped as she walked, for all the world as though she were strolling through the graveyard on a fine summer's morning with nothing more sinister in mind than to say a pious God-Help-Us at the church altar. From the shadow of trees and bushes and headstones, nine pairs of eyes watched her, and eight throats hissed in soft outrage through lattices of clamped fingers. Only the beldame was silent; though she smiled the cold, grim smile of vindication, for with the wisdom of her great age and great experience she had known the truth. She knew, too, that her cohorts were watching her, and slightly but emphatically she shook her head, warning them to make no move. Not yet, the gesture said. Not yet.

First, the flowers went. Leah gathered them up in armfuls, wreaths and posies alike, flinging them aside to expose the bare earth of the grave, damp and loose still from the day's rain. Then the headstone. The beldame was greatly impressed: who would have thought such a scrawny slip of a thing had such strength in her? Over the stone went with a heavy thud. Then Leah began to dig. Quick and eager as a terrier scenting a tantalising rat, her hands wielded the spade and the soil flew in all directions. And Leah began to sing another song. A shrill, excited song of love and desire and longing; a song to Carolan that told him she was here, she was coming to him, breaking through to take him from his lonely bed and carry him home, where she would be his wife for ever more. Laughter bubbled between the song's eerie phrases; the spade flashed, the earth flew.

And the beldame raised her stick in the prearranged signal that told the women to leave their hiding places and close in.

When Carolan's gammer spoke her name in a tone like the wrath of God himself, Leah shrieked. The spade dropped from her hands into the deepening hole, and her head came up, face deadly white, eyes huge and round and staring.

Nine figures formed a circle around her, a circle from which there was no escape. Nine faces glared back at her, vengeance glittering in their eyes. Nine mouths pronounced curses and anathemas, naming her blasphemer and desecrator and unholy serpent. And nine pairs of hands reached out —

"No." Leah's voice was high-pitched and so strange, almost childlike, that it made them pause. "Oh no, oh, *no*," she giggled. "You'll not touch me, you see! You can't touch me, you see! He's

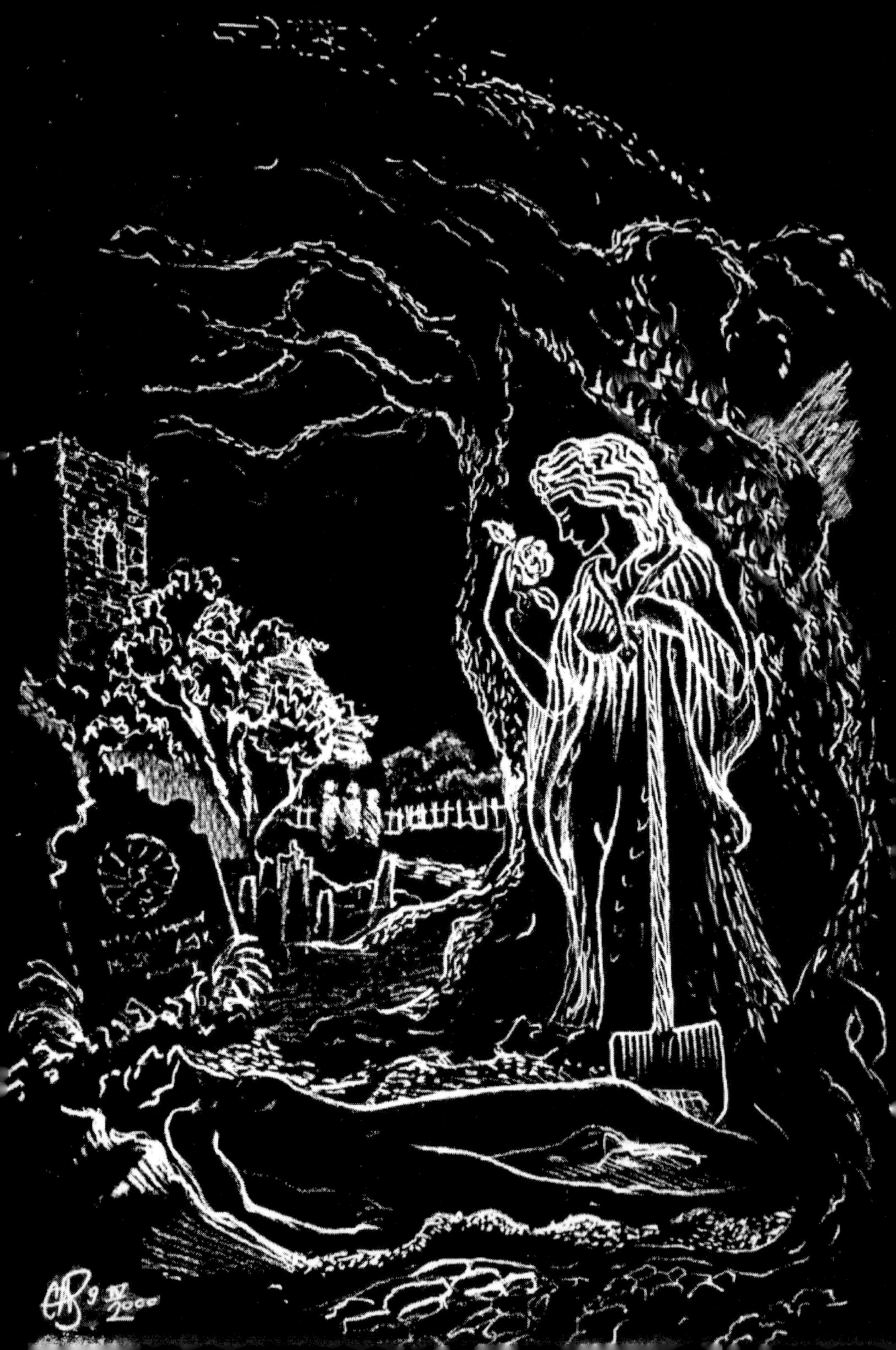

mine — Carolan's mine, just as he always was. And I've come for him now, I'll take him now, I'll take him *home!*" Didn't they understand? Fools, they were — they must be *made* to understand! "Ignorant old women, what do you know?" she cried "I can bring him back! I can make him alive again! I know the magic, you see. Mammati showed me the magic, long ago, long, long ago, in the woods, in the night, while you all snored in your beds!" Wildly her head swung, her crazed eyes raking them all. "See, look!" Her fingers clawed dramatically. "I'll turn you all into *things!* Slugs and snails, so the toads will eat you! Gnats and fireflies, so the bats will swoop down and snap you up! So I can and so I will!"

But they knew the truth, and even in her madness Leah saw it then. The blacksmith's wife and the wheelwright's wife and Carolan's mother and all the others, staring, unmoved, unafraid. And presiding over them all like a carrion crow, the beldame herself with her stick of blackthorn wood and with the certainty of Leah's fate in her eyes.

The blacksmith's wife stood nearest to the desecrated grave. She turned, stooped, and picked up the spade Leah had dropped. Then she smiled, and slowly, steadily, the women began to close in.

Only the beldame didn't advance, for her sharp old eyes had seen a flicker of movement by the lych-gate, the flutter of a priestly robe betrayed by the moon. She spared one glance for the other women, just enough to be assured that all was at it should be, then moved away from the closing circle and hobbled towards the gate.

"Ah, grandmother..." Father Borlagh's voice quavered just a little, though his brows frowned sternly down at her. "What do you do here tonight?"

The beldame smiled a smile that made the blood trickle like dust in his veins. "Nothing that is the concern of priests or men, good Father."

"This is God's holy place!"

"Indeed it is, and God's justice will be done here." A hand, a claw, reached out to pat his arm. "Go you home now, Father Borlagh. Go you home and say your prayers, and leave women's work to the hands of women. All will be finished before morning."

The priest watched her as she limped back towards the small, silent circle by the graveside. He knew he should follow, but he could not. At this moment no man, if he was wise, would dare to follow where the beldame trod. He turned at last and walked slowly away. And as he went, he heard the sounds begin. Sounds like the muffled beating of drums in steady, inexorable rhythm, as eight staves and one long-handled spade rose and fell, rose and fell, rose and fell, in the moonlit churchyard.

✦ ✦ ✦

Leah opened her eyes to see starlight glittering among the boughs of the yew tree far above her head. For a few moments she remembered nothing, and then she remembered everything, and with a small cry – which her ears did not hear – she tried to sit up. Something seemed to hold her back – then suddenly there was a sensation as of tearing and she found herself standing on her own feet and gazing down at what lay in the grass where she had awoken...

The beldame and her ewe-flock had done their work well, and there was no blood to stain this hallowed place. Only a broken, boneless doll, discarded now and left behind to lie beneath the yew tree.

Leah said: "Oh..." And then she began to understand, and she said, "Oh, yes. Oh, *yes*..."

The women were gone, back to their hearths and their menfolk, their lips sealed. Father Borlagh was gone to the shelter of his house and his close-drawn curtains, and would utter no word of what he had seen. Leah giggled, though the sound was beyond the hearing of any human soul. Oh yes, oh *yes*. They had shown her the way, and now at last she knew what she must do.

The grave was whole again, the headstone upright, the flowers lovingly replaced and nodding their frail heads in the night breeze. No breeze moved Leah's hair and skirt as she stepped to the graveside and knelt down. She sang Carolan's name, three times three. And at the last singing she closed her eyes and felt the land around her slip away, far away, as she gave herself to the call of another and more terrible world.

And he was there, as she had known he would be, asleep in the dark and only waiting. She touched his face with fingers light and insubstantial as cobwebs, and he woke, and he saw her.

"Carolan." The thing that Leah had become spoke tenderly as a mother to her new-born child, and her fingers caressed his cheek, his hair, his breast. "Ah, Carolan."

He tried to make a sound, an inarticulate cry of fear, of horror. Then his lips formed Calla's name.

"No, no, my dear one. Calla is far away. You have no use for her now." She pulled him to her, pulled him from the shackles of decaying flesh and browning bone, and she held him in her arms, though he cried and pleaded to be set free, to sleep the dreamless sleep again. She smiled and let him weep. She would be patient, for in time he would learn to accept what she had granted him. Here in the dark, beyond the reach of prayers, she would teach him. All would be well now. All would be well.

"Ah, Carolan," she whispered again. "Did you think I would forget? Did you think I would leave you? I have come to you, Carolan. I have come to find you. And I'll be with you now, my love. I'll be with you now for all eternity. I will be your true and only wife..."

THE FOUR SEASONS ARGUE WITH THE OAK SPIRIT

THE BIRTHDAY BATTLE

Most of the best stories begin with "Once upon a time". However, the thing that was happening in this story didn't just happen once. In fact, it had happened every year for the past four thousand years, which when you think about it is a lot of "upon a times".

The thing in question was a birthday. For the grand old Yew that was the oldest tree in Wych Wood was soon to be four thousand years old. That sort of birthday is, of course, a very special occasion indeed, and all the inhabitants of the wood agreed that a grand celebration should be held. They would have liked to ask the Spirit of the Yew, who lived deep in the tree's ancient trunk, exactly what kind of celebration he would best enjoy. However, that presented a problem – because Yew Spirit was asleep, and would not wake until the birthday itself arrived.

Perhaps I should explain a little about the reason for this. Most trees live to a very great age given the chance, and Yew trees are among the longest-lived of all. When Yew Spirit was young, Stonehenge had only just been built; and by the time Julius Caesar came to conquer Britain, Yew Spirit was downright middle-aged. These days, he was what the creatures of Wych Wood politely called an elderly gentleman, (though this annoyed the Elder trees, who found it confusing). Elderly gentlemen like to sleep a lot, and Yew Spirit was no exception. Since the reign of King Alfred (the one who burnt the cakes) he had slept a very great deal, and now he woke up only once every hundred years, to celebrate special birthdays.

So, as they could not wake Yew Spirit to ask him, the inhabitants of Wych Wood gathered together to decide for themselves what sort of festivities to put on. There was a great deal of argument, which the older creatures, like the Oak Spirits and one particular Tawny Owl who claimed to be over a hundred years old (though no one believed him), said it was only to be expected. The songbirds' and bees' suggestion of a grand concert was objected to by creatures who could only sing badly or not at all, while the ants' idea of a marching display, together with a fly-past by the Gnat and Midge squadrons, was scorned as being much too dull. The voles squeaked excitedly that everyone should do everything they could, all at once and very fast. But no one listened to them. No one ever did.

Before long the argument started to get out of hand, and at last the being who was, so to speak, chairing the meeting (though actually he wasn't sitting on a chair, but on the knee of Oak Spirit's tree) clapped his hands and called for order. As he did so, a cloud scudded across the sun and there was a flicker of lightning and grumble of thunder. Everyone promptly fell silent — even the voles stopped squeaking, which was a very rare thing indeed.

"That's *better.*" Summer, who was one of the four Seasons and who was dressed in sky-blue and had hair as yellow and mellow as ripe corn, smiled at the company. The cloud cleared, the thunder stopped, and there was a scent of roses in the Wood. "Now, perhaps I can make a suggestion of my own?" Summer continued. "After all, this is *my* Season," he waved a hand around, indicating the flowers and the green canopy of leaves and the warm air buzzing with insects, "so we should plan something with a summery theme. Also, it seems to me that all the suggestions that have been made so far aren't very original. We *always* have concerts and marching displays and so on for Yew Spirit. I think this time we should do something different."

The other creatures looked at each other.

"Sounds sensible to me," said a badger, gruffly.

"We like the idea," chimed in the wild flowers.

"Defzzzinitely," agreed the bees.

Then from the shadows between two tall Sycamore trees a new voice, that sounded like a stream chuckling, said, "*Ha!*"

Everyone turned round in surprise as, with a rushing, dancing breeze, a newcomer appeared. She was dressed in the palest green, and her hair was the colour of daffodils, flowing over her shoulders like water. Skipping into the middle of the clearing, she looked around, then put her hands on her hips and said, "Well? What are you all staring at? Anyone would think you'd never seen me before!"

Summer jumped to his feet, outraged. "What do you want, Spring?"

Spring stuck her tongue out at him. A shower of rain pattered down through the leaves overhead. "I've come to make the arrangements for Yew Spirit's birthday," she said.

"But this is my Season, not yours!" Summer protested. "You've had your turn – go away, go back to sleep!"

"Ha!" Spring said again, and tossed her hair. "There's my dear brother for you – trying to keep me away from the biggest party Wych Wood has ever seen!"

"But you can't come! It isn't the right time of year!"

"Then perhaps it should be," Spring said crossly. "I've been listening to you going on and on about doing something original for Yew Spirit – well, what's *really* original is to change the Season to mine!" She clasped her hands together and twirled round. "Spring, with the sap rising in his branches, and all his tiny flowers full of golden pollen, and the weather just right for him. Not boring, dusty Summer when he gets hot and dry and uncomfortable and pestered by more insects than he can shake a branch at—"

"Hey!" the caterpillars and earwigs protested. "Do you mind?"

Spring wrinkled her nose and ignored them. "What *I* say," she continued, "is that we should have a Spring festival. Then Yew Spirit can—"

She got no further, for another voice interrupted her. "And who, sister Spring, says that you know what's best for Yew Spirit?" With another lively gust of wind, a brown-haired figure whose gown rustled like fallen leaves and whose cheeks were as rosy as ripe apples appeared among them. Several squirrels yawned, and a cluster of leaves abruptly turned brown and fell, much to the surprise of the Hazel tree who owned them.

Autumn, for that was the new visitor, gazed graciously around and said, "Well, this is a pretty gathering! And what about *my* part in the celebrations? Yew Spirit is very fond of my mellow and peaceful

Season; he has said so on many occasions."

Summer and Spring exploded furiously together. "He's done no such thing!" Summer cried, and "Ha!" snorted Spring yet again.

"Scoff if you like," said Autumn in a superior tone, "but everyone knows that *I* am Yew Spirit's favourite Season. I am a time for dreaming, and for thinking of pleasant things. I am the Season in which Yew Spirit can relax, be comfortable, settle down—"

"And what, Sister Autumn, follows that settling down? Answer me that!"

The air turned so cold that every single creature in the wood shivered. And Winter, tall and thin and stately, with frost-silver hair and a beard like icicles, stood among them.

Three hedgehogs curled themselves up into prickly balls and hibernated on the spot. A stoat (whose fur had suddenly turned white) nudged them, but only hurt his paw, and the hedgehogs flatly refused to unroll. Winter frowned sternly at everyone, but most especially at Summer, and said, "Yew Spirit likes *my* Season best of all. I bring him peace and comfort, the cold that cleanses his roots and branches. The chance to rest and sleep."

"He's done nothing but sleep for the past hundred years," Summer interrupted sourly. There was another flicker of lightning. "And when he does wake up, he certainly won't want to see the land all freezing grey and white, without a scrap of colour anywhere. Face the truth, Winter. You're *boring*."

"Until you get in a bad temper," said Autumn huffily. "Then you make life miserable for everyone."

"Yes," Spring agreed. "You don't know *anything* about peace, Winter! Gales, blizzards, sleet . If you knew the mess I have to clear up after you every year—"

"You're a fine one to talk about mess!" Summer growled. "You and those floods you're so fond of! And with you, it's hot one moment, cold the next. You can never stick to anything for more than five minutes!"

"Well, you can all argue as much as you like," Winter announced. "But *I* know what Yew Spirit would like, and *I'm* going to make sure he has it." He drew himself up to his full height, and the sky turned to the strange, pink-tinged-purple colour that heralds snow. "When Yew Spirit wakes, it will be Winter!"

Fat, cold, white flakes began to drift down from above. The flowers squealed and hid, pulling their heads and their leaves under the earth. Squirrels bolted for their dreys, the insects fled, and all the hedgehogs in Wych Wood fell sound asleep.

"Now, wait a minute, Winter!" Summer shouted — or rather stammered, for his teeth were chattering. "You can't just walk grandly in here and take over! This is *my* Season!"

"Well, it shouldn't be," said Autumn, whose apply cheeks looked a bit pinched now. "And it shouldn't be *his*," glaring at Winter, "or *hers*," with a scowl at Spring. "Yew Spirit wants *me*!"

Spring cried, "HA!" again, but this time so loudly that the smaller creatures blocked their ears. The snow turned to rain, soaking everyone. Clumps of snowdrops and daffodils appeared, shaking their heads in puzzlement, and several hedgehogs woke up, mumbling, "Whazzat? Whassgoingon?"

"Now, *look*!" said Summer. The sun came out. The snowdrops and daffodils said, "Please will you make your *minds* up!" as the dog-roses jostled them out of the way, while the hedgehogs started snuffling for something to eat.

Autumn opened her mouth to protest, but before she could say a word Summer continued. "It's perfectly simple," he told the other Seasons. "I have a right to be here, and you don't. So you can just go away until it's your proper time to wake up. Go on, all of you. *Shoo*!"

"Listen to him," sniffed Autumn.

"La-di-da!" Spring stuck her tongue out again.

"You can't make me go away," said Winter with a sly smile. "I'm stronger than you are."

Summer said, "Ha!" then scowled, annoyed that he had caught the habit from Spring. "Prove it."

"I shall."

"And what about us?" cried Spring and Autumn together. "We're strong — we can beat you both!"

"I can beat you all," added Autumn.

Spring pulled a hideous face at her. "Can't!"

"Can!"

"Can't!"

"Can, so there!"

The creatures of Wych Wood had so far listened in uneasy silence, but at last Oak Spirit felt he couldn't keep quiet any longer. "Ladies, gentlemen, *please!*" he beseeched. "You mustn't quarrel like this... it's very confusing for the rest of us, you know." Which indeed it was, for at that moment the Oak tree had buds, acorns and bare branches all at once, and couldn't decide whether his roots felt cold and soggy or hot and thirsty.

Autumn turned and looked at him in annoyance. "Keep out of this," she said. "It's none of your business."

"But it is," Oak Spirit protested, and from his topmost branch Tawny Owl hooted agreement. "*We* were the ones who wanted to arrange a welcome for Yew Spirit, and I think we should have some say in the matter."

"Nonsense," said Winter. "What do you know about it? You're only a tree."

Under Winter's withering stare, all Oak Spirit's acorns and remaining leaves fell to the ground with a *whump*. A group of voles, who were underneath, squeaked in protest, and Oak Spirit said sadly, "But this squabbling is getting us nowhere."

"There I agree with you," replied Winter. "So there's only one thing for it — Spring and Summer and Autumn and I must challenge each other to battle. And the winner will be the one to greet Yew Spirit when he wakes on his birthday."

The creatures of Wych Wood looked at each other in dismay. They were already having a taste of what happened when the Seasons quarrelled, and a full-scale fight didn't bear thinking about. But when they turned to Summer for help (after all, it was his rightful Season, as he had said), they saw that Summer was getting quite keen on the idea.

"Right, then," he said briskly. His eyes sparkled blue as a cloudless sky and a wave of heat went through the wood, melting the icicles that now hung from poor Oak Spirit's branches. "I accept your challenge, Winter."

"But—" pleaded Oak Spirit; and, "Oh, *no*..." groaned the other creatures. The Seasons ignored them. They were all excited now.

"Let's not waste any more time," said Winter. He raised one finger as if it was a starting-gun. "On the count of three... One, two, three... *go!*"

So the Birthday Battle began — and such mayhem and chaos had never been known in Wych Wood before. As Tawny Owl said later, it was like trying to live four different lives all at once; and he freely admitted that he didn't have it half as bad as some of the other creatures. Take the squirrels, for instance. One moment they were curled up sound asleep in their dreys while a blizzard raged outside; then suddenly Autumn got the upper hand and they were racing hither and thither in a frantic search for nuts to hide away; only there weren't any nuts, for the next instant it was Spring and there were a baffling number of young, green shoots to nibble. The birds were in a tizzy of confusion. Swallows and swifts and cuckoos were puffed out with starting on their long flights southward, only to find themselves turning round in mid-air and coming back again every five minutes. And the rest complained that it was no fun to be feasting happily on a lovely Autumn glut of blackberries and elderberries and rowan-berries, then seconds later to find the berries gone and the whole nuisancy business of nest-building starting all over again when they'd only just taught the last clutch of fledglings to fly.

The plants had the worst of it. The trees sprouted brown leaves, green leaves, catkins and a layer of snow all together (and a heavy weight that added up to, they grumbled), while bluebells and anemones were buried by showers of beech nuts, and the summer flowers got frostbite. Some creatures, such as the hedgehogs and dormice (there were a few dormice in Wych Wood, though they tended to keep themselves to themselves), simply gave up, found quiet corners to hide in, and snored through the whole thing. But for most of the inhabitants, the Battle was a time to be remembered; and one which they would have much preferred to forget.

At last, at Oak Spirit's urging, Tawny Owl called an emergency meeting in the clearing where the first gathering had taken place. It was late; in fact it was nearly midnight, and this had been the most confusing day of all, for Sun had set early, only to pop up over the horizon again as the freezing, wintry afternoon turned into a balmy summer evening. Now, Moon rode high in a cloudless sky scattered with stars, while snow fell thickly (how snow could fall out of a cloudless sky no one knew, but no one had the energy left to ask). And it was hot.

As many creatures as could turned up to the meeting. Most, though, were either too tired or too dizzy with the constant switching and swapping, so it was a fairly small and sorry company that gathered in a half-circle at the Oak tree's feet. Oak Spirit gave his report, but it wasn't a happy one. All his efforts to make the Seasons see sense had failed, and now they wouldn't even speak to him. Nor, he added, was there any sign that any one of them would ever win the battle, for they were all too evenly matched.

A badger, who had been enjoying a meal of fallen crab-apples until they suddenly vanished right under his nose, looked up and blinked through the snow. "But that's awful!" he said. "If none of them can win, then this disorder will just go on and on for ever!" He frowned, staring suspiciously at the place where the crab-apples had been. "I don't *like* disorder."

"None of us likes it," said Oak Spirit, ignoring the voles who started to squeak that they didn't mind. "But as to how we can stop it... I have to confess I'm stumped."

"Tree-stumped?" asked a magpie with a chattering laugh, but no one else appreciated the joke.

"The trouble is," Oak Spirit went on, "we need the advice of someone older than we are. Someone who might remember if anything like this has ever happened before, and so would know what to do about it." He sighed. "We thought of asking Sun — after all, he's been around longer than anyone. But when the skylarks flew up and tried to talk to him, he only sulked and told them to go away and not bother him until all this silliness stopped."

A vixen with a bedraggled tail (her cubs kept getting Spring fever and biting it) spoke up. "If Sun won't help us, what about Moon? She's nearly as old as he is, and very wise."

Oak Spirit hadn't thought of that, for the sky had been in such a muddle since the Battle began that Moon had hardly been seen. Tonight, though, she was out.

"Well..." Oak Spirit said, "we could *try*..."

"Vixen could ask her," Tawny Owl put in. "She does her best barking by Moon's light. And I do my best flying by Moon, so I'll go with her."

Everyone agreed that this seemed a good idea, so Vixen and Tawny Owl set off to the edge of the wood, from where they could call to Moon without the trees getting in the way. The others waited for them to come back, shivering one moment, fanning themselves and panting the next. A nightingale started to sing, but gave up when icicles formed on her beak.

At last a flutter of wings and a rustle in the undergrowth announced the return of Vixen and Tawny Owl.

"What happened?" they were asked eagerly. "Did Moon answer you?"

"Oh, she answered," said Tawny Owl. "She isn't sulking; in fact she doesn't seem the least bit bothered by any of it. But she wasn't much help."

"She just said, 'what will be, will be'," added Vixen with a sniff, and cuffed a cub who tried to pounce on her twitching tail-tip as a clump of daffodils popped up beside her.

"Fat lot of use I call that," grumbled Badger. "So *now* what? Anyone else got any bright ideas?"

It seemed no one had, for an embarrassed silence fell. Vixen and Tawny Owl were disappointed at their failure. Oak Spirit and all the other trees were deep in thought. Then, just as one of the voles was about to open his mouth and suggest that maybe "if everyone ran round and round in circles, very fast and all at the same time, it might..." there was a sudden change in the air. Change was hardly unusual now, of course, and they were all thoroughly sick of it – but this was *different*. For the air in the Wood grew very, very still. And there was a feeling of... *something*... about to happen. Something very... *important*...

Tawny Owl was the first to suspect the truth. His eyes opened very wide and he said, "Does anyone know... what time it is?"

They didn't for sure, but the Badger abruptly realised what Tawny Owl was getting at. "I think," he whispered, " that it could be just about midnight..."

Midnight. A new day. And today was —

There came a soft, deep rustling, the sound of thousands and thousands of tiny, green needles moving gently together, and a strong, heady, resiny scent wafted through Wych Wood. Slowly, fearfully, the gathering turned their heads to look. And there in the heart of the Wood, where the shadows were at their darkest, they saw him. He was gnarled and stately, with the oldest and wisest eyes that anyone had ever seen, and he sat high up in his tree, where the great trunk had divided into three, as though he were a king seated on a throne.

The day of the birthday had come, and Yew Spirit had woken from his hundred years of sleep.

"Children, children!" Yew Spirit's voice was slow and strong and awe-inspiring. "It is good to see you all again."

"Yew Spirit..." Oak Spirit's voice was filled with respect, even though it felt very strange to him to be called a child. "We... we had planned a special welcome..."

"To wish you a happy birthday," added Tawny Owl.

"Yes. Yes, happy birthday! Um... "

"And many happy returns, of course. Oh, dear..."

Then, like a storm breaking, every single creature at the gathering started babbling at once as they all tried to tell Yew Spirit what they had meant to do and how everything had gone so horribly wrong.

"Spring started it! She—"

"But Summer was as bad, because he got all excited about the challenge and—"

"They won't even talk to us!"

"We're freezing!"

"Boiling!"

"Hungry!"

"Sleepy!"

And at last, in one great chorus. "*We're fed up!*"

"*Children!*" Yew Spirit's voice rushed through the Wood like a huge, soft gale, and instantly the clamour stopped. A vole squeaked, once, but one of the wood-ants nipped him before he could do it again. "I understand what has happened," Yew Spirit continued. "Sit still, all of you, and stop worrying. I will deal with this Birthday Battle!"

He drew a vast breath, and called out, "SPRING. SUMMER. AUTUMN. WINTER. I AM AWAKE!"

With a warm, whirling breeze that made the exhausted daffodils struggle above ground yet again, Spring came dancing into the clearing. "Welcome, Yew Spirit!" she cried delightedly. "See; your favourite Season is here to greet you!"

"Oh no you don't!" another voice shouted, and a yellow-haired figure rushed in on her heels, brandishing a long strand of honeysuckle with which he tried to trip her up. "Happy birthday, Yew Spirit! It's Summer, the Season you like best!"

"*I* am the Season Yew Spirit enjoys!" cried Autumn, running at Summer and pelting him with conkers so that he yelped. "Hello, Yew Spirit — welcome to your special day!"

"Silly fools, with your frivolous games!" roared Winter, marching into the clearing with a swathe of crackling frost behind him. "Greetings, noble Yew Spirit! I am here to bring you the solemn peace you desire!"

The four Seasons started to argue again. They shouted at the tops of their voices, they threw things at each other, they stamped their feet with rage, until the whole of Wych Wood quaked with their quarrelling. Moon, still floating high above it all, said, "Well, *really!*" but no one heard her above the din. And even Sun came out of his sulk and peered in astonishment over the horizon.

Then Yew Spirit's voice rang out once more.

"STOP THIS AT ONCE!"

To the surprise of all the woodland creatures, the Seasons did stop, and stood very still, looking at Yew Spirit. Spring pouted and tossed her hair. Summer looked ashamed of himself. Autumn's cheeks were very, very pink. And Winter put his hands behind his back and whistled a little tune, as if the row had been nothing to do with him.

"I am ashamed of you all," said Yew Spirit sternly. "This is supposed to be a celebration, not a fight! And it is most certainly *not* the kind of birthday I want!"

The Seasons shuffled their feet. "We only thought..." Autumn began.

"I know what you thought, and you are all extremely conceited," said Yew Spirit. "Why should I prefer any one of you to the others? I enjoy every Season — but only at its proper time. And the creatures of Wych Wood agree with me." Squeaks, rustles, barks, twitters and buzzes of agreement followed this.

"But," said Winter, "we thought that as this is such a special birthday, you should choose which Season you wanted. Just this once."

"Then why didn't you wait until I woke up, and ask me?" demanded Yew Spirit.

"Um..." said Winter. He didn't have an answer to that.

Yew Spirit sighed. "All right. I see that you meant well, so I *shall* choose. Do you agree to abide by my decision?"

"Oh, yes!" the Seasons chorused. "We promise!"

An odd little smile appeared on Yew Spirit's gnarled face. "Then I choose... *none* of you."

Their faces fell. "What?" said Summer; and, "You can't do that!" protested Spring.

"Oh, I can. Don't argue. You promised, remember? You can't break a promise. So — go away. All of you. Now!"

The Seasons looked at each other in dismay. Then, all together, they vanished.

And here, the story does become just *once* upon a time. As the four disappeared, the strangest, eeriest and most awful thing that had ever happened in Wych Wood took place. For suddenly, there was no Season at all. That is very, very hard to imagine, but I'll try to describe it as best I can. It wasn't at all cold, yet it wasn't at all warm. It wasn't really dark, but then again it wasn't really light. There wasn't any rain; yet somehow there wasn't any dry, either.

No leaves or flowers; yet no snow or frost. No buds. No fruit. No birdsong, no chuckle of water, no squeaking voles; no sound whatever. Everyone felt tired; yet no one could sleep. There was just... *nothing* in the whole of Wych Wood.

The creatures of the Wood looked slowly and fearfully around. What they saw frightened them. It wasn't natural. It wasn't *right*. At last, Tawny Owl dared to turn his head towards Yew Spirit, and spoke in a quavering voice.

"Please, Yew Spirit... we don't like this..."

"Of course you don't," said Yew Spirit gently. "And I won't make it last. I just wanted to teach those silly, squabbling Seasons a lesson, and I think they've learned it now." He raised his voice and called out to the still, grey, *nothing* air. "ALL OF YOU. COME BACK."

The Seasons appeared one by one. They, too, had seen what had happened, and their eyes were as wide and frightened as the eyes of the woodland creatures.

Spring whispered, "We're sorry. We didn't mean..."

"It was my fault," mumbled Winter. "I started it."

"The rest of us were as bad," said Autumn.

Summer only stared down at his own feet, until Yew Spirit spoke again. "Say a friendly goodbye to your brother Summer," he told the other three. "This is his Season, and the rest of you must go back to sleep until your proper turn comes."

Spring started to look sullen and a single daffodil appeared at her feet. Yew Spirit frowned warningly. Spring shrugged, and with a sigh of relief the daffodil vanished again.

"Goodbye, Summer," said Spring. She kissed his cheek, and vanished.

Autumn said, "Just one branch of crab-apples, Yew Spirit...? Badger was so enjoying them... Oh, very well. Goodbye, Summer. I'll be back to take over from you." And she too kissed him and was gone.

Winter was much too dignified to kiss anyone, so he just bowed stiffly, and said, "I wish you well, brother Summer. Goodbye."

Then only Summer was left. And the relief that the creatures of Wych Wood felt as the air grew warmer, and the leaves sprang to life, and the honeysuckle and dandelions and roses and mallows and valerians and all the other flowers of the proper season appeared, was so enormous that they felt they would burst with it. Young birds in their nests clamoured for food and started trying their wings. The bees hummed contentedly. The fox cubs stopped biting their mother's tail and chased each other instead. The hedgehogs woke up. And the voles, of course, started to squeak with all the energy they had.

Later, Yew Spirit thought, he would have a quiet word with Summer. Not in front of the others, for it would be unkind to embarrass him in public. But he would make quite sure that Summer had learned his lesson, and that he would be especially kind to Wych Wood this year. First, though, there was something else to be settled, and he called the creatures around him, hushing their eager thanks for coming to their rescue.

"If you want to repay me," he said, "then what about putting on a splendid birthday celebration? What did you have in mind before all this trouble started?"

The creatures looked at each other. "Er..." they said. And: "You see, we were just going to decide, when..."

"I understand," said Yew Spirit. "Well, how about a nice concert from the songbirds and bees? And you ants — I know how much you like marching, so why not show me your best display? If the gnats and midges want to make a fly-past, too, that will please me enormously. And the sight and sound of all the voles running around and making as much noise as they can is *very* enjoyable."

As Yew Spirit continued to list the things he would like — which were exactly the same things that the creatures of Wych Wood had done for four thousand years — Oak Spirit and Tawny Owl wished that they had been able to arrange something original for this very special occasion. But then they thought of the Birthday Battle, and how it had started... and they decided that perhaps it was just as well they hadn't.

ST GUMPER'S FEAST

"Come on," Richard said. "Only another few yards, and we're there."

"*Metres*, Dad," Keren corrected scornfully. "We use *metres* now."

"You use what you like; as far as I'm concerned, it's yards and always will be." Richard stubbed his toes on another barnacle-encrusted rock and bit back the word he would have liked to say. He wasn't in the mood for teenage angst, and Keren had been sulking now for upwards of three hours. She didn't like St Gumper, and why did her lousy parents have to choose it for a holiday, and if they *had* to come to Cornwall why couldn't it at least have been Rock, which was cool, though not as cool as the Caribbean where her best friends were going this year, and it wasn't fair, and why did everyone set out to make her life so *boring*?

Lydia was too far ahead of them to overhear her daughter's complaints. Not for her the teetering and frequently painful scramble over rocks whose sole aim in life seemed to be to cause maximum damage to human feet and shins; with the largest bag of beach kit under one arm and Charlie, their eight-year-old, hanging on to the other, she was as sure-footed as a cat. Charlie wasn't complaining about St Gumper. Far from it. To him, anywhere that had sand to dig in, sea to splash in and rock pools to fish and fiddle around in was heaven on earth. It had been his idea to leave the main beach and climb across this rock outcrop to the second beach around the headland, and Richard and Lydia had been happy enough to indulge him. The second beach was much smaller, and the holidaymakers who had already settled there were mostly family parties, suggesting

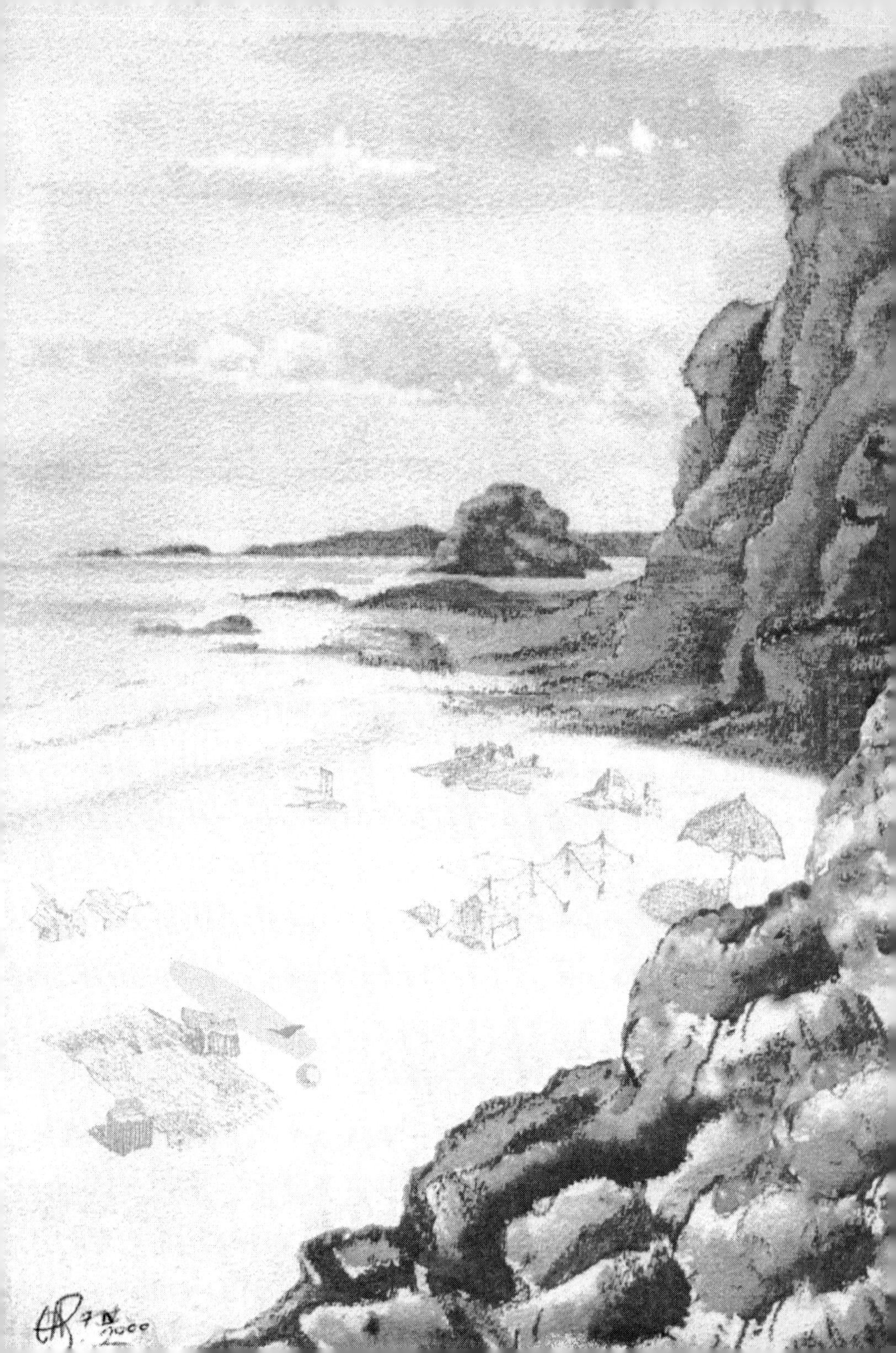

that it was a better and safer choice for children, and worth the effort it was taking to get there.

Lydia and Charlie negotiated the last of the rocks and reached smooth sand, and by the time Richard followed, Charlie was already racing towards the beach's far end, fishing net tightly grasped. Richard dumped his own burden of rolled towels and picnic coolbox and paused to get his breath, while Keren, with a martyred face, struggled the final yards (metres?) to join him.

"I *hate* it here!" she informed him tragically.

"Good," said Richard. "Doing things you hate is a valuable lesson in life." He was scanning the beach for a suitable spot to spread themselves, working out which way the sun would track so that they wouldn't be shaded in an hour or two. Once he was settled, he had no intention whatever of interrupting his sunbathing for anything other than food.

Lydia saw him looking and called to him, pointing. "There, where that rock juts out. We can see the whole beach and keep an eye on Charlie."

He signalled acknowledgement, picked up his baggage again and trudged over the sand, which was very white and fine and felt pleasurably hot under his feet. This mini-heatwave was a bonus for England at any time of year, and the weather forecasters said it was set to last for at least a week. By the time they left, Richard told himself, he'd have a tan to rival anything he could have got in Keren's lamented Caribbean.

He was surprised by the number of people on the beach. St Gumper wasn't exactly on the beaten track of holiday destinations; they'd only discovered its existence through an obscure website on the Net, and the small enclave of self-catering chalets that they'd booked in to was the sole option for any visitors who wanted to stay. Even on the map it was hard to find; a tiny cove tucked away among miles of otherwise inaccessible coastline, with the village's name printed in the smallest type imaginable. It had promised to be the perfect get-away-from-it location, and on their arrival yesterday Richard and Lydia hadn't been disappointed. The village had two shops, three pubs and a wonderfully tranquil atmosphere, and the main beach was wide and unspoiled. Visiting the most picturesque of the pubs last night, Richard had also found the local regulars very friendly, with none of the hostility towards tourists (they called them "emmets" here, apparently) that popular mythology had led him to expect. Oh, no, one old boy had said; visitors were always welcome. Part of the furniture now, you might say. Plenty came back more than once, and a few had even settled here — retired, that kind of thing — and become part of the locality. St Gumper couldn't get along without them, and nobody minded admitting it. New life, that was the secret of a thriving community. New life, new blood. That sort of thing.

At their designated spot, Lydia spread the larger of the two rugs out on the sand. Charlie was already poking his net into the crevices of a nearby rock pool, and Keren had plonked herself down at a pointed distance and, back to her parents and face in hands, was staring glumly at the sea.

Ignoring her, Lydia said, "We won't need the windbreak, will we? There's hardly a breath."

Richard was inclined to agree; though there were quite a few windbreaks, sun-umbrellas and like paraphernalia dotted about. In fact, almost every party on this beach had put up some kind of barrier, as if they had all set out to enclose themselves in little private fortresses that were not to be breached by strangers. The Englishness of it all made him smile, and a sixty-something woman sitting in an old-fashioned deckchair a short way off smiled back.

"Lovely day," she said. The accent was Home Counties and the clothes what might be described as Postwar Holidaymaker; flowered button-through dress with a full skirt, shirt-style collar and capped sleeves, with sensible peep-toe sandals to complete the effect. Even her hair matched: short, and looking as if it spent most of its time being strangled by ferociously tight rollers. Old-fashioned eccentric, Richard told himself. Her husband (presumably) sat in an adjoining chair, which had been raked back to its lowest angle. He had a handkerchief over his face and appeared to be sound asleep.

"Lovely," Richard agreed. He walked towards her, out of politeness. "Quite a bonus for the English summer."

She laughed. "Oh, we usually have our share of heat around St Gumper's Feast. We're well known for it."

He noted the *we;* and also her healthy tan, which hadn't been acquired in a short space of time. "You live here, do you?"

Her nod had a hint of smugness. "First came down on holiday more years ago than I care to remember. Then Geoffrey retired, and when we came again, we stayed. Marvellous place. Marvellous." She glanced in Keren's direction. "Though your daughter doesn't seem to think so."

Richard laughed wryly. "She wanted to go to Barbados."

"Ah well; they're all the same at that age, aren't they? She'll learn." Another, faintly mischievous smile caught at the edges of her mouth. "Maybe St Gumper's Feast will put her in a different frame of mind."

That was the second time she'd referred to St Gumper's Feast, and from an obscure corner of Richard's mind a recent memory rose. "Someone in the Cutter Inn mentioned that last night... it's today, isn't it?"

"Tomorrow, strictly speaking. Today's St Gumper's *Eve*; but they tend to overlap."

"Ah. Right. So there really was a St Gumper?"

"Oh, very definitely," said the woman. "Mind you, we don't know much about him, other than that he was a hermit of some sort. Most of them were, I think, and some of the Cornish saints are particularly obscure. But he was certainly real."

Richard nodded. "So what happens at St Gumper's Feast?"

"Not a lot. They make a bit of a thing of it in the Cutter and the other pubs. Oh, and a party on the beach tonight. Only a small one, for us locals. You know the form, I expect."

Richard didn't, but nodded again. The husband, under his handkerchief, made a snorting noise then settled back to silence. "Well..." Richard said, "I'd better help my wife with the beach kit. Nice to talk to you."

"Absolutely," the woman concurred. "What do those Americans say? 'Have a nice day'. That's the expression, isn't it?"

As he returned to where Lydia was still unpacking, Richard noticed that the other beach-goers in the vicinity all seemed to be looking at him. Their interest was casual but noticeable, and for a moment he felt faintly uneasy. But when he tried a few experimental smiles, everyone smiled back pleasantly enough. Probably it was his winter-pallid skin that attracted attention. He and his family seemed to be the only people on the beach without tans; everyone else looked as if they had spent their entire lives basking in summer sunshine. Ah, well. A few days, and he'd catch them up.

Lydia had changed into her bikini and was sitting on the rug with a small yellow booklet in her hand.

"Tide table," she explained, waving it. "According to this it's low tide in half an hour, then another hour on the turn before it starts coming in. We'll have to be a bit careful. Those rocks are the only way back, and I imagine the water covers them at high tide."

A muscular young man sitting within earshot peered out from under an enormous sunshade. "It does, luv," he said, in a voice that sounded just like the Cheeky Cockney Chappie beloved of old Hollywood films. "Once the tide's half way in, you can't go back over them."

"Ah." Richard squinted up at the cliffs rising like bastions behind them. Lydia was right; there was no other way off the beach. "Then we can't spend all afternoon here. Pity."

The young man laughed. "S'all right; you don't need to go over the rocks. Use the tunnel."

"Tunnel?" said Lydia.

"Up there." He waved vaguely at the rock face. "Straight through the cliff and you're back in the village. Didn't anyone tell you?"

Richard and Lydia both shook their heads.

"Oh, right. You must be staying at the holiday park, then. They're useless at givin' out information. Yeah; the tunnel's been there centuries. There's a legend says old St Gumper dug it with his bare hands. Ha!" The young man laughed explosively. "*That*'d've took a miracle, wouldn't it? But whatever, you just go through it, so you can stay on the beach till the sea gets to the last patch of sand. No problem."

Lydia said, "Thank you," and added under her breath to Richard,

"Another resident?"

"Mmm." Richard was still scanning the cliff, but couldn't see anything tunnel-like in its craggy face. There were some rough steps slanting at an angle, but they appeared to stop at a ledge no more than six feet up. The ledge curved away round a craggy buttress and the tunnel entrance was hidden from this angle. Anyway, if it came down to it, they only had to take their cue from the other beach-goers, and leave when they left.

The young man had turned away and buried his nose in a magazine. Near his feet, his two very small daughters were building a rickety sandcastle. They were quaint, chubby little things, in swimsuits with gathered skirts, and with floppy cotton sunhats pulled firmly down over their ears. Richard watched them for a few moments, then realised that he was staring and looked away.

He rummaged in the bags for his swimming trunks, found them and was changing under a towel when Keren came slouching to the rug, dragging her feet and looking melancholy. "I'm hungry," she stated. "Is there anything to eat?"

Lydia looked up. "Cold chicken and coleslaw, or—"

"I *hate* coleslaw! And chicken's so *naff*."

"Well, I got some Cornish pasties from the shop—"

"Oh, God, *no!*"

Lydia sighed wearily and Richard said, "We've got what we've got: put up with it or go without."

Keren gave him a searing look. "I'll have to starve, then, won't I?" She waited, and when no sympathy was forthcoming added petulantly, "Where's my Lycra? I *suppose* I might as well sunbathe."

Richard opened his mouth again but Lydia gave a warning shake of the head and he subsided. Keren slathered herself with tanning oil and flopped sullenly face-down on her towel, and Charlie came back from his explorations full of tales of *huge* fish and *gi-normous* crabs. The sun shone in a cloudless sky. The waves rose and fell and creamed on the tideline, their ceaseless noise soothing, where the (almost) similar background of the city traffic they had left behind was not. Children laughed and shouted; gulls mimicked them with their screams. Richard put on his sunglasses and shook out the daily paper for a leisurely read. All was right with the world. Absolutely.

❖ ❖ ❖

Sun, sand, sea and happy sounds. Richard read the paper from cover to cover, then realised that he was hungry. Lydia had taken Charlie down to the sea's edge and Keren, too, had gone off somewhere, so he didn't wait for them but opened the coolbox and laid out the picnic. He ate a pasty and half a bar of fruit and nut chocolate that already had sand in it, then turned to look out to sea. A sharp little breeze played catspaw on his face and chest, and he noticed that a small rock which had been on dry sand when he settled down now had water lapping at its further edge. Tide had turned, then; it was almost a yard (*"metre!"* he mentally heard Keren saying) closer. He must have taken longer over the paper than he had realised.

He looked around, but none of the other beach-goers were showing any sign of moving or packing up. In fact most of the little fortresses were deserted and there was quite a crowd down at the water's edge, paddling or splashing in the sea. Odd how they all seemed to congregate in the same spot at the same time, as if some hive instinct had drawn them there. Even the sixty-something Home Counties woman had tucked her flowered dress into her bloomers, or whatever she wore underneath, and was standing in the shallows, legs akimbo, like Canute. Her husband slept on under his handkerchief, but he was almost the only human being, bar Richard himself, left on the sand.

He looked for Lydia and Charlie but couldn't pick them out from among the milling shapes and colours against the background of sun on water. What he saw instead was the angular shape of Keren coming up the beach towards him. She avoided his eyes and threw herself down on her towel without a word.

Richard said, "Where are your mother and Charlie?"

Keren shrugged. "How should I know? In the water somewhere, last time I saw them." Her own swimsuit was wet, but only to the waist. Clearly the sea wasn't to her taste, either.

Suddenly Richard did pick Lydia out, and a moment later saw

Charlie a few paces from her, playing with two other boys of about his own age. Irrationally, he felt a stab of relief, followed by an equally irrational twinge of guilt that he hadn't been keeping an eye on them. That surprised him: he wasn't normally given to what Lydia would call old-fashioned chauvinistic impulses; and besides, she was a better swimmer than he was, more practical all round, in fact. It would never have occurred to him to consult a tide-table, for example—

Keren interrupted his train of thought. "Dad, I'm so *bored.* Do we *have* to stay here all day?"

"Yes," said Richard.

"Ohh*hhh*..." She clenched her fists and pressed them to her skull. "But I want to *do* something!"

"There's plenty to do. Swimming, sunbathing, reading. Or you could help Charlie make a sandcastle."

"Kids' stuff. Oh, great!" Keren sighed with the weariness of a saint tried beyond endurance.. "Can't I go back to the village?"

"No, you can't." Knowing her, Richard thought, she'd probably try to hitch a lift to the nearest town that had a video hire shop. "You can stay here till we all go, then come back with us."

"But I don't *want* to! Dad—"

"I said, *no.*"

He thought she would argue (she usually did), but instead she turned her back on him and then stood up. Nonchalantly and obviously casual, she started to saunter towards the cliffs. The ploy was obvious. She had overheard the earlier conversation about the tunnel, and she intended to find it and sneak off that way. Well, let her try. He'd warned her, and if he had to go after her and make a scene in front of half the beach, the fault, and the embarrassment, would be hers.

Richard watched Keren as she walked slowly away. He would give her a chance to do as she was told, but only one. She reached the rough-cut steps, glanced back (he pretending to be absorbed in his paper) then climbed up to the ledge and vanished round the buttress. Right. If she didn't reappear in five seconds...

But she did, tossing her hair back as though to imply, *nothing there, and even if there was, I wouldn't be interested.* Richard smiled dryly. For all her bravado, Keren didn't yet have the confidence — quite — to openly defy her parents. He'd won this tussle, and he was satisfied. To save Keren's face he didn't wait for her but rose and walked down the shore as she approached. Lydia was still talking to her new acquaintance; seeing him she waved and he went to join her.

"Hello, love." Lydia had obviously been swimming; her hair was plastered against her neck and shoulders and beads of water glittered on her skin. She indicated her companion. "Meet Molly. She moved here too — ten years ago, was it, Molly? This is my husband, Richard."

"Pleased to meet you." Another unCornish accent; she was from Lancashire. "Lydia says it's your first time in St Gumper."

"That's right. We'd never even heard of it until two months ago." Richard smiled, but accompanying the smile came a sudden and unexpected feeling of discomfort. He couldn't put a finger on it, but there was something about this woman that didn't quite gel. He wouldn't go so far as to call it a *wrongness*, but...

"Molly's been telling me about this feast day," Lydia said, unaware of Richard's reaction. "The party tonight sounds like fun. Even Keren might force herself to enjoy it."

"Great." Richard wasn't concentrating. What *was* it about Molly that troubled him...?

"We'll come along, then, yes?"

"Sure. Yes." Still he couldn't place it, but the discomforting feeling was getting stronger. Abruptly, without knowing why, he asked, "You've been here ten years, you said?"

"Something like that," Molly said cheerfully. "Thirty-sev... what am I talking about; *twenty*-seven when I came here. Divorced, dead-end job, nothing to keep me where I was..." She grinned wryly.

"And you like it?"

"Oh, yes. It changed my life, and that's a fact."

"For the better, presumably?"

She looked surprised. "Yes," she said. "Of course."

At that moment, the anomaly that had been baffling Richard clicked into place in his mind. It was Molly's hair. The cut of it, the style, even the colour (which wasn't natural). It was pure 1980s. All right, that was hardly a world ago, but even at a distance of ten or twelve years it looked extraordinarily dated. You simply didn't see people with styles like that any more.

Lydia was saying something and he hadn't taken it in, so when his brain caught up with the last two words "...shall we?", he floundered.

"Er... yes," he said, hoping it was the right response. "Why not?"

"Come on, then." She started to wade into the sea. "And you can meet Charlie's new friends and their parents." She smiled at the other woman. "Bye, Molly. See you tonight."

"Grand." Molly smiled back. "Nine o'clockish. I'll be here."

She waved, a waggling of her fingers, then strolled away along the water's edge. "Come on!" Lydia said again to Richard. "Race you to that rock over there!"

He realised belatedly that the thing he had unwittingly agreed to was a swim, and wished he hadn't. But Lydia was already thigh-deep, and as a wave came breaking towards her she threw herself into it, water shattering up as she disappeared. The wave foamed over Richard's legs, splashing his torso, and he breathed in sharply with the cold shock of it.

"Softie!" Lydia had surfaced, bobbing on the swell. "It's great once you're in!"

Oh, sure, he thought, and felt a momentary sympathy for Keren and her Caribbean yearnings. Bracing himself, and with teeth clenched, he took a short run at the deeper water and flung himself forward, striking out after his wife as she headed for the rock.

Lydia won the race, as he had expected; she was like a seal whereas he, though he could keep going, was slow and methodical. He managed to bark his shin on an underwater projection, and swore as he trod water, trying to ignore her amusement.

"We ought to keep an eye on Charlie," he said.

Lydia shaded her eyes against the glare and looked back along the beach. "He's all right. Still playing with his new mates; I can see him."

"All the same." He didn't know why but he wanted suddenly to know what kind of children his son was befriending; to observe them, talk to their parents. The impulse didn't make a lot of sense, but it was powerful and he could not ignore it.

They pushed themselves away from the rock, and Lydia kept pace with him as they swam slowly back. Near the tideline, Charlie and the two boys were messing around with something black that, as Richard stood up in the shallows and was able to see more clearly, proved to be an inflated inner tube. He was surprised. With beach toys of every imaginable shape and colour on sale in all the seaside shops, something as basic and old-fashioned as this looked out of place.

Basic. Old-fashioned. Dated. The words hung around in his head like wisps of smoke that wouldn't quite dissipate, and he turned to Lydia.

"What are those boys' names?"

She looked at him curiously. "I'm not sure. Does it matter?"

"No." Richard frowned. "Of course not. I just wondered..."

"Now you mention it, they're both called something a bit odd, I think," she said. "You know — unusual; not used much these days. Hang on — Ronald, that's one. And the other's... Alfred, or something like that." She smiled. "Maybe those sorts of names are coming back into fashion again. But I bet they won't thank their parents for it when they get older."

One of the boys was indeed Ronald, and the other's name was Freddie, though short for Frederick rather than Alfred. They were extraordinarily polite children, and to Richard's astonishment called him "sir". They wore baggy shorts rather than swimming trunks, and as with Molly, their hair was downright peculiar; cropped very short at the back and around the ears, with a fringe in front that looked as if it had been cut round using the rim of a pudding basin. As for their parents... London to the core, they were a pleasant enough couple, the husband thin and angular with several teeth missing, the wife plumper and sporting a truly dreadful shade of bright orange lipstick. They, too, had moved here — "So much safer for the kiddies, what with everything that's going on up London these days" as the wife put it — and they, too, talked about St Gumper's

Feast and in particular the party on the beach.

"The tide'll be going out again nicely by then," the husband informed Richard, nodding to emphasise his words. "Get the old fire started — bangers, chops, nice bit of bread and marg and some beer to wash it all down with."

"Then a sing-song," said his wife. "We always finish up with a sing-song, don't we, Ron?"

Another Ronald then, and they'd named their elder boy after him... that, too, was something that didn't happen so often these days. *Old-fashioned. Dated...* Richard was more than uncomfortable now. He was distinctly uneasy.

He made excuses to leave them as soon as he could, calling Charlie a little sharply from his games and leading him and Lydia back to their spot on the sand. Keren was awake and looked up at their approach.

"Some boy came up and started talking to me just now," she said. "He was really weird. Asked me if I was *courting!*"

"Where is he?" Richard looked quickly around.

"I told him to piss off, so he did."

"I've told you before, don't use that word!" But Lydia wasn't really concentrating on Keren. "Richard, what's the matter with you?"

Richard gave up his futile search for Keren's would-be admirer and turned his gaze to the London family, still at the sea's edge. "Them," he said under his breath.

"Who? Ron and his wife?"

"Yes. And the others. All of them." He swung round to face her. "Oh come on, Lyd, you must have noticed!"

"Noticed what?"

"They... they're all..." He flapped a hand helplessly, unable to find the words that would express exactly what he felt. "They're all so weird."

"Glory be!" said Keren sarcastically. "Dad's actually *noticed* something!"

"What are you talking about?" Lydia turned on her. "Don't be so ridiculous, of course they're not weird!"

Keren said, "Oh, aren't they?" and Richard sighed. "I don't know how to describe it, but... take a look around. A *good* look. Hair, clothes, mannerisms. Ron and his wife are the most obvious, but the others have all got it, too."

"Got *what,* for Christ's sake?"

"That... old-fashioned look. As if they belong to another age. It even shows in the way they talk."

Lydia began to look a little dubious. "Well, this is an old-fashioned place, isn't it? It's probably like 'the village that time forgot', you know. Hasn't moved on with the rest of us."

"Oh, come on! There's nowhere left in England that's *that* isolated! Honestly, Lyd, there's something strange going on here, I'm certain of it."

Keren had sat upright and was listening intently. Suddenly she said, in a tone that had none of her customary petulance, "I agree with Dad. And I think we ought to go."

Richard threw a grateful glance at her. "So do I."

Lydia put her fists on her hips and stared at them both in turn. "What is this, some sort of a wind-up? You two are crazy — I think the sun's got to you both!" She dropped her hands and shook her head, as if shaking off a cloud of irritating midges. "Look, Richard, this is the first day of our holiday, and we've got glorious weather and a lovely beach, and I am *not* going to spoil it for the sake of some silly piece of paranoia! There's *nothing* wrong with St Gumper *or* the people who live in it. All right, they're a bit old-fashioned, I take your point, but you can put it down to eccentricity from living in a small rural community."

"That's patronising, Mum," Keren objected.

"Oh, be quiet! It isn't anything of the sort; it's simply the truth. Now look, I am going to sit down, and enjoy my lunch, and then I'm going to sunbathe. If you two want to go somewhere else that's up to you, but Charlie and I are staying *put!*"

There was no point in arguing with Lydia in such a mood; her stubborn streak, as Richard's father had once observed, was a mile wide and as solid as steel. Richard could only watch helplessly as she made herself comfortable on the rug and started to lay out the contents of the coolbox for a full-scale picnic.

Keren said: "Dad ... *we* don't have to hang around..."

It was tempting... but Richard pushed the idea away. "No," he replied. "I think we'd better stay." Reason struggled to make itself heard. "Your mother's right. There's nothing going on. There can't be."

And if there was, he added silently to himself, then he could hardly take Keren away and leave the rest of his family to face it alone.

❂ ❂ ❂

Lydia and Charlie demolished the picnic, but Richard was no longer hungry. He felt restless, like a soldier on watch, and every few minutes he was driven by some inner compulsion to get to his feet and patrol the length of the beach. He couldn't have said what he was looking for, and he observed nothing that he could class as truly suspicious. But the unease remained, and nothing could banish it.

He also kept an eye on the tide, which was now encroaching by clear degrees on the sand. When the first surges began to touch the rocks that divided them from the main beach and the village beyond, he glanced quickly back, half expecting to see the beginnings of a mass exodus. But the idyllic scene was unchanged. Chairs and sunshades and windbreaks stood undisturbed; the sea was fringed with tanned, happy people. Shouting and laughter drifted to him on the breeze. He could even see Charlie, back with his new friends and trying to use the inner tube as a boat. No one showed any sign of leaving. They would all use the tunnel; of course they would.

Perhaps, he thought, that was at the root of what troubled him. The tunnel, reputedly as old as Gumper (even if the saint hadn't dug it with his bare hands), was the only way off the beach once the sea covered those rocks. It was nonsensical, but the prospect of being accompanied by the villagers through what might prove to be a long, dark and utterly unfamiliar walkway gave him the creeps. If there *was* anything amiss, what better place than the tunnel for it to show itself?

Well, that was easily dealt with: they'd simply leave before anyone else did. Nonetheless, Richard decided that it might be a sound idea to take a look at the tunnel entrance for himself. Just to get an idea of it, and know what to expect. Lydia would laugh, but he needn't explain to her. It would set his mind at rest if nothing else.

Lydia, however, pre-empted him as he tried to tiptoe past on his way to the steps.

"Darling..." She was lying prone on the rug, and no longer annoyed with him. "Put some more sun-oil on my back, will you?"

Thinking (not for the first time) that she must have eyes in her back of her head, Richard complied. Keren was sunbathing too, and seemed to have fallen asleep; leastways she didn't move a muscle. As he smoothed the last handful of oil over Lydia's skin, Charlie came back from the water, dripping over everything. He sat down and yawned hugely. "I'm tired!"

"Have a nap," Lydia suggested.

"Might. Where's my comic?"

"Wherever you left it. Probably under your clothes."

Yawns were catching, and Richard felt his own face muscles tugging into a wide stretch. His legs were aching, too, with the unfamiliar exercise of walking barefoot on sand. Maybe he'd sit down for a bit before checking the tunnel. The tide had a good way to go, so there was plenty of time.

Lydia settled with a contented sigh, face pressed into her cushion. He looked at the sea. At the bathers and paddlers. They all looked so happy and (at this distance) normal that the idea of anything being awry seemed suddenly as nonsensical as Lydia said it was. Charlie's nose was in his comic, Keren was snoring faintly. Richard smiled. He'd tell her about that when she woke up: she'd be livid.

He put his sunglasses on and lay back.

❂ ❂ ❂

When he woke, both the breeze and the angle of the sun had markedly changed. Richard sat up in a disorientated flurry; his glasses fell off, bouncing on the rug, and for a moment the light's glare blinded him. When the dazzle cleared, he saw two things that turned him cold.

The tide's edge was less than three yards from his feet. And there was no one in the water any more.

"Ye gods!" Twisting, Richard reached out for Lydia, who still slept on, with Charlie also fast asleep beside her. "Lyd, wake up, *wake up!*"

"Uh?" She stirred and raised her head, blinking. "What is it?"

"They've gone! They've all gone off the beach and left us here, and no one said a *word* about..."

He stopped, staring as his brain registered the third shocking thing. Spreading away along what was left of the beach was a bright array of towels, rugs, windbreaks, sunshades... All the beach paraphernalia of the hot day, still there, untouched, undisturbed, only waiting for its owners' return.

Yet, apart from themselves, there wasn't a soul in sight.

Richard scrabbled to his feet and looked wildly in every direction. *Nothing.* The beach was deserted; no figures in the distance, not a sound of a human voice, the sea empty. Even the old man who had spent the day somnolent under his handkerchief was no longer there.

"*Damn* them! Bloody locals — I suppose they think it's funny, leaving us to it and sneaking off! Let the emmets get all their things soaked, have a good laugh at our expense!" He was nearly shaking with rage, and with something else, something he didn't want to acknowledge, that made him overreact.

Lydia had sat up now and was staring at the two empty deck chairs a few feet away. Her face oddly blank, she said, "But they've left *their* things, too..."

"What?" Then abruptly the wrongness of that hit Richard with a painful mental thump. The villagers wouldn't simply have gone away, not without taking their belongings. No one would. It didn't make *sense*.

Keren woke then. She propped herself on her elbows, started to say, "What are you two arguing—" and the words broke off as she saw the situation for herself. "Oh, shit..."

For the first time in her life Lydia didn't warn her about bad language. She was still staring at the bizarre, deserted scene, and her face had lost most of its colour. "Charlie." There was an edge to her voice. "Come on, Charlie, get up. We're going." She snatched up the coolbox, started to stuff things haphazardly into it.

Keren looked up at her. "Going?" she repeated hollowly. "How, Mum? *How?*"

"Through the tunnel of course, how else?" Lydia snapped. "Look at the rocks — they're completely under water! No one could get over them now!"

Keren said, "What tunnel?"

"The one in the cliff, the one that man told us about!" Lydia paused and glared angrily, though the anger wasn't specifically directed at her daughter. "Weren't you listening? We go up those steps, and along a ledge at the top—"

Keren said: "There's no tunnel there."

"What do you mean, there's no tunnel? Of course there is, the man said so! We just—"

"Mum, there *isn't!*" Keren's face had turned a sickly shade. "I know, because I *looked!* Dad —" She turned in desperate appeal to Richard. "You saw me, didn't you? I went up there..."

And I assumed she was being obedient, a voice in Richard's head whispered. *She wasn't. She didn't go, because there was nowhere to go. No tunnel. No way out. Nothing...*

Suddenly he was running, sprinting for the rough steps, scrambling up them, clawing his way to the top. There was a ledge; oh yes, there was a ledge, and it led round a jutting outcrop, to —

A blank wall, in the face of an unscaleable cliff.

His family were waiting for him to reappear, their faces all turned up to him, pallid and expectant. Richard did not need to call out to them. He just shook his head with a slow movement that killed the sparks of their hope. When he reached the sand again Keren was crying and Charlie on the verge of it, though he hadn't grasped the enormity of their situation. Richard tried to say something — he felt somehow that it was his duty and responsibility — but words refused to come. There was nothing he *could* say.

Finally Lydia broke the silence. "How high..." She swallowed, aware that her voice was unnaturally shrill and trying to control it. "How high do you think the water comes?"

Richard had thought of that, and on the way back down the steps had seen the telltale signs; the delineating mark between barnacles and vegetation. He didn't want to answer but knew he must.

"High enough," he said.

"Even on the ledge...?"

A nod. "The cove narrows, you see. Forms a bottleneck, so it'll surge that much more. And above the ledge the cliff's sheer." He paused. "There's no way, Lyd. Not unless we can—" He gave a peculiar, hiccuping laugh and wiped his mouth with the back of one hand. "Unless we can all learn to breathe under water pretty bloody fast..."

Lydia didn't flinch or shout at him, understanding and possibly even sharing the need for crassness at a moment like this. For perhaps a minute, perhaps more, they all stood like abandoned puppets, neither moving nor speaking. Then:

"Maybe they'll come back for us," Richard said. "The villagers..."

Lydia's mouth twitched in a grimace. "How? If there's no tunnel."

He felt foolish. But there had to be *something*. To be standing here on an English beach, on a beautiful summer afternoon with the sun blazing in a cloudless sky and the sea a perfect picture of blue water and white-crested breakers... it was like a scene from a holiday brochure.

Except that in less than two hours, they would all drown.

Scraping the barrel of desperation now, he tried again. "If we shout — someone might hear—"

Lydia and Keren both gave him such scornful looks that he turned away, stinging with embarrassment. Sure, someone might hear. But there would be no call to the nearest coastguard or lifeboat station, and no marine equivalent of the Seventh Cavalry appearing over the horizon to their rescue. Nor did they have any ropes, or wings, or a magic bottle with an obliging genie in it. He'd even made Keren leave her mobile phone back at the chalet, and if he called himself every kind of dictatorial cretin under the sun there was no point in being wise after the event.

Richard looked at the sea, and hated it with a loathing that he hadn't known he was capable of feeling. All that shining, inviting, invigorating beauty: come to the seaside, enjoy the clean air, get away from it all... they were certainly going to do that, weren't they? Get *right* away. And there would be no coming back.

He made a choked, ugly noise and, to hide the fact that there were tears of terror in his eyes, walked the few paces to the edge of the incoming tide. He'd be all right in a minute or two; just needed to get himself back under control and then he could be of use to his family again. Only he *was* no use, for there was nothing he could *do*. He thought disjointed thoughts about at least putting Charlie up on his shoulders so that maybe, just maybe... But it wouldn't be enough and it would only prolong the inevitable. What was drowning like? A dire, battling agony, or a peaceful slipping away? It wasn't something he had ever thought about. Well, you don't, do you? Hardly in the everyday run of life. Now, though -

"Richard." Lydia's voice cut into the meandering fog that his mind had become. There was a quiet decisiveness in her tone and it surprised him into turning to face her again.

"There's only one chance," she said, coming down the beach to meet him. "I'm going to try to swim back to the village."

He was horrified. "You can't! It's too far — and the currents, the rocks—"

"Richard, don't be so ridiculous!" There was a wild look in Lydia's eyes. "If we all stay here we're going to drown anyway, so worrying about things like currents is *insane!* It *is* our only hope, however small it might be!" She hesitated, eyeing the sea obliquely. "I'm a strong swimmer. I think I can do it. It's just..."

"What?"

Her throat muscles moved convulsively. "I suppose I'm thinking that... that if it doesn't work, we should all have been... together."

"I know." Richard spoke softly. "But I'll look after them. Right to the last."

She nodded, and he moved to a discreet distance as she called Keren and Charlie to her and put an arm around both, talking quickly and quietly. Then she ran back to Richard, kissed him — he hadn't been kissed like that in quite some time — and said, "I love you. Don't ever forget that."

"I won't." His voice caught, and he couldn't control it properly. "I love you. And we'll see you soon."

"One way or another." She managed a wan smile. "Wish me luck, then."

"Break a leg!" he said.

"That's for actors, not swimmers." But she still just held on to the smile. And then she was wading into the sea, diving, surfacing, and swimming away with steady, powerful strokes.

Richard watched the bobbing sphere of her head and felt as if the world was collapsing with the weight of all the things he could and should have said to her before he let her go. Tears were streaming down his face when someone moved beside him and a hand slipped tentatively into his, gripping his fingers.

"You're not religious, are you, Dad?" Keren said.

Richard bit his lip. "No..."

"Nor me. But I sort of... feel like... I don't know." She shrugged, turned her head aside. "Praying, or something."

Richard squeezed her hand. "You do that, love, if you want to. Do anything that feels right."

She nodded. "Charlie doesn't understand what's going on. He wants me to make a speedboat for him out of the sand."

"Maybe it'd help him." Richard was still watching Lydia; Keren, it seemed, didn't want to look. "Or you."

"Maybe. Dad..."

"Yes, love?"

Keren hesitated, then shook her head. "Nothing. It doesn't matter."

※ ※ ※

Half an hour gone. Richard had strained his eyes until he could no longer fool himself that Lydia was still visible, then watched his children as they made Charlie's speedboat. He found himself greedy for every tiny detail of their behaviour; voices, movements, the flop of hair, the turn of light and shadow on their bodies. Keren was wearing Lydia's sweater and jeans, as if they somehow kept her in

111

contact with her mother. Charlie was still in his trunks.

The speedboat was only half completed when the sea reached it. Charlie pouted at the first wet collapse, but Richard gave him no time to think about it.

"Come on." The tide was moving much faster now; another few minutes would see it touch the cliffs. He started to shepherd Charlie towards the steps. "We'll find another game to play."

"When's Mum coming back?" Charlie demanded. "I want to go home!"

"All right." Richard scanned the empty sea. "She'll be back soon, and then we can go."

They went up the steps in single file. It occurred to Richard how shallow the climb was; at the top, they were barely six feet higher than they had been on the sand. The sun had shifted further westward and dropped, and its light gave a deceptively gentle slant to the lengthening shadows. It was still warm. Richard didn't look at his watch. He did not want to know the time. Time was a mechanical, clumsy, human concept and it no longer had any meaning.

The ledge was in shade and the surrounding rock looked shabby and faintly dangerous. Charlie was sensing something of the prevailing mood now and began to get whiney; "Dad, I don't like it here any more! Where's Mum? I want *Mum!*" Richard couldn't answer him, for the same question was burning in his own mind but with an ugly, adult immediacy. Where *was* Lydia? In the village now, dizzy with exhaustion, picking her painful, barefoot way from the bigger beach towards the nearest phone box, crying, praying... Or drifting like a stray strand of kelp in the sea's shifting currents, eyes wide but seeing nothing, mouth open but no longer breathing, spiralling down, dying, dead...

An hour gone. Yes, he had looked at his watch, because there was nothing else to do that might add to his store of knowledge. The sea had covered the foot of the cliff and the water level was rising rapidly. Looking down (not pleasant, but he made himself do it) he saw it biting angrily at the rock a mere couple of feet below him. There was a strongly defined swell now. You could see the danger in it, imagine the foolish arrogance that could tempt a man to think he was stronger than it was and lead him to challenge its power. *But Lydia was a good swimmer. She was. She **was**...*

Half an hour more. The sun vanished from the little cove, sliding beyond the headland that bordered the covered rocks. The breeze became stronger, with the hint of an evening chill to it. They sat on the ledge; Keren huddled in a foetal position in the crook of Richard's left arm, while Charlie, bored, but silenced by some subliminal awareness of trouble, made desultory patterns with one finger in the thin, dry layer of sand.

Keren said; "She didn't make it, Dad. Did she?"

Richard couldn't answer. He was watching the sea again.

"Dad." She pinched him, quite hard. "We're going to die, aren't we?"

He didn't mean to do it and it was the last thing he had wanted, but he turned on her. "*Shut up!*" His voice was high-pitched, savage. "You and your *stupid* questions — I don't *know* what's going to happen; I don't know *anything* any more, and if you think—"

He stopped, gasping, as realisation of what he was doing caught up with him. Keren didn't speak. She only looked at him, her face crumpling, and in her eyes he saw the complete betrayal of the belief she had had, until this moment, that somehow he and Lydia would make everything come right.

Richard jerked round, turning his face back to the sea.

And saw the sudden splashing disturbance some twenty yards out.

"Oh, God..." His hands gripped the rock behind him. "*What's that?*"

Keren saw it too, and would have fallen off the ledge if he hadn't reflexively grabbed at her. "It..." Her torso heaved. "Dad, it's..."

Then, where the splashing had been, what looked like a human head rose and broke surface. Keren's eyes bulged wide with incredulous hope... then her expression began to change...

Not one head but two. Richard could see them more clearly now. They were both dark-haired — Lydia was fair — and they were bobbing towards the shore. Reaching shallower water, they stood up, and Richard saw that they were dragging something else between them. They looked up at the ledge, and he recognised them both. Ron, and Molly. Ron raised a hand; a cryptic gesture, waving but with something else implied. Then they began to wade towards him, and as they came closer he saw what their burden was.

"Sorry, mate." Ron met Richard's horrified eyes with the coldest and most calculating look he had ever seen. "Game girl, your missis. But she weren't quite up to it."

"It's the currents," Molly added. She sounded sympathetic; she did not look it. "They're very strong round here, and I don't suppose anyone told her, did they?"

Behind them, the sea's surface churned again, and more heads rose. Six — eight — ten: Richard found himself counting them, as if doing so was his only possible chance of holding on to his sanity. Ron's wife. Their two sons. The cheeky-cockney-chappie with his well-developed muscles. The home-counties woman, her husband, wide awake now and smiling pleasantly beside her. Others. *All* of them...

He said nothing. He did nothing. He only watched, frozen as if in a dream that he couldn't control, as Ron and Molly heaved Lydia's body up to the ledge and laid her, with a care that bordered on the obscene, at his feet. Keren and Charlie were statues, staring, their eyes as blank and uncomprehending as their mother's blue, dead gaze.

"Sorry," Ron said again. "Bad luck, eh? But don't worry, mate; it's happened to all of us. Over the years." He glanced at his wife. "Forty-two, that was us, weren't it, Midge?"

The orange-lipsticked woman nodded. "S'right. Only came to get the kids away from the Blitz. Funny old world, eh?"

"Yeh," Molly agreed. "Nineteen-eighty-five, me."

"And we were the summer of fifty-one," added the Home Counties woman briskly. "Unforgettable. Quite unforgettable."

Molly smiled at Richard. "We'll see you later, then. After the tide turns, for the party, right?" She started to back away down the steps. The Home Counties woman waved.

"Ta-ta for now," said Ron. He dived. Molly followed, and the others, all of them, sank beneath the surface of the water and were gone.

Richard stood on the ledge, looking at the sea. He felt as if he had become one with the cliff; granite to the core, unchanging, unfeeling, immovable. A part of his mind that seemed to belong to another person and another world was aware of his children's presence, but they too were no more than rock. Nothing had any meaning. Nothing at all.

Molly's words echoed distantly in his mind. *See you later.* All of them. Same place, same date, every year... world without end, amen. Happy feast day, St Gumper...

Hidden behind the rampart of the cliffs, the sun moved inexorably towards the northwestern horizon. The sound of the sea was stronger now as the tide funnelled in faster and the water level continued to climb.

Soon, the cove was empty.

BIBLIOGRAPHY

Novels:
The Book of Paradox (1973)
Lord Of No Time (1977)
Blood Summer (1976)
In Memory Of Sarah Bailey (1977)
Crown Of Horn (1981)
The Blacksmith (1982)
Mirage (1987)
The King's Demon (1996)
Sacrament of Night (1997)
Our Lady of the Snow (1998)
The Summer Witch (1999)

The *Time Master* **trilogy** (expanded from *Lord of No Time*):
The Initiate (1985)
The Outcast (1986)
The Master (1987)

The *Chaos Gate* **trilogy** (sequel to *Time Master*):
The Deceiver (1991)
The Pretender (1991)
The Avenger (1992)

The *Star Shadow* **trilogy** (prequel to *Time Master*):
Star Ascendant (1994)
Eclipse (1994)
Moonset (1995)

The *Indigo saga*:
Nemesis (1988)
Inferno (1988)
Infanta (1989)
Nocturne (1990)
Troika (1991)
Avatar (1991)
Revenant (1992)
Aisling (1993)

Pseudonymous Novels:
As Elizabeth Hann:
Walburga's Eve
As Anna Stanton:
Journey's End
Dangerous Desire
The Rose of Jaipur
Sea Song

Young Adults and Childrens Fiction:
The Thorn Key (1988)
The Sleep of Stone (1991)
Firespell (1996) (republished as *Heart of Fire*)
The Hounds of Winter (1996) (republished as *Heart of Ice*)
Blood Dance (1996) (republished as *Heart of Stone*)
The Shrouded Mirror (1996) (republished as *Heart of Glass*)
Heart of Dust (1998)
Daughter of Storms (1996)
The Dark Caller (1997)
Keepers of Light (1998)
Storm Ghost (1998)
Mirror, Mirror 1 - Breaking Through (2000)
Mirror, Mirror 2 - Running Free (2000)

The *Creatures* Series: (1998-2000)
Once I Caught A Fish Alive
If You Go Down To The Woods
See How They Run
Who's Been Sitting In My Chair?
Atishoo, Atishoo - All Fall Down!
Give A Dog A Bone
Daddy's Gone A-Hunting
Incy Wincy Spider
Here Comes A Candle
Creatures At Christmas (short story collection)

Selected Short Fiction (adult & childrens):
 'The Birthday Battle', *The Mammoth Book of Fairy Tales*,
   ed. Mike Ashley, Robinson (1997)
 'Cry', *Other Edens III*, ed. C. Evans & R. Holdstock, Unwin (1989)
   The Glass Slip-Up, The Mammoth Book of Comic Fantasy,
   ed. Mike Ashley, Robinson (1998)
 'His True And Only Wife', *Realms of Fantasy* (April 1995)
   Not Wisely, But Too Well, Shakespearean Whodunnits,
   ed. Mike Ashley, Robinson (1997)
 'The Spiral Garden', *Realms of Fantasy* (Aug 1997)
   Tithing Night, Tales from the Forbidden Planet, ed. Roz Kaveney (1987)
   Realms of Fantasy (August 1997)
 'St Gumper's Feast', *The Spiral Garden*, ed. Jan. Edwards, BFS (2000)

Stories with bite!

Creatures

Incy Wincy Spider

Louise Cooper

Louise Cooper

SCHOLASTIC

OTHER PUBLICATIONS FROM

SHOCKS by Ronald Chetwynd-Hayes.
A collection of four spine-chilling stories from Britain's Prince of Chill. £6.00 (60pp A5 chapbook).
SIGNED COPIES AVAILABLE WHILE STOCKS LAST

LONG MEMORIES by Peter Cannon.
A memoir of the life and final days of Frank Belknap Long, a contemporary and friend of H P Lovecraft. £5.00 (68pp A5 chapbook).
SIGNED COPIES AVAILABLE.

MANITOU MAN:
THE WORLDS OF GRAHAM MASTERTON
by Graham Masterton, Ray Clark and Matt Williams.
A collection of ten short stories, plus keen critical analysis and a complete bibliography to the work of best-selling author Graham Masterton. £7.99 (240pp A5 paperback book).
SIGNED AND NUMBERED LIMITED EDITION.

CLIVE BARKER:
MYTHMAKER FOR THE MILLENNIUM
by Suzanne J Barbieri.
Analysis of Barker's work, concentrating on the mythological aspects and also his handling of female characters. £4.99 (62pp 'B' format paperback).
SIGNED COPIES AVAILABLE.

HOLT! WHO GOES THERE? by Tom Holt.
A collection of sketches, articles and musings from top humorous fantasist Tom Holt. £4.99 (48pp A5 chapbook).
SIGNED AND NUMBERED LIMITED EDITION.

To order please add 50 pence postage and packing per item, and send a cheque or postal order for the total amount (overseas orders please write for further details) to:

BFS Publications,
c/o 3 Tamworth Close, Lower Earley,
Reading, Berkshire, RG6 4EQ

The British Fantasy Society
http://www.herebedragons.co.uk/bfs

There is a group of people who know all the latest publishing news and gossip. They enjoy the very best in fiction. They can read articles by and about their favourite authors and know in advance when those authors' books are being published. These people belong to the British Fantasy Society.

The BFS publishes fantasy and horror fiction, speculative articles, artwork, reviews, interviews, comment and much more. They also organise the annual FantasyCon convention to which publishers, editors, authors and fans flock to hear the announcement of the coveted British Fantasy Awards, voted on by the members.

Membership of the BFS is open to everyone. The annual UK subscription is £20.00 which covers the Newsletter and the magazines. To join, send moneys payable to the BFS together with your name and address to:

**The BFS Secretary,
c/o 201 Reddish Road,
South Reddish, Stockport,
SK5 7HR**

art by Wayne Burns

Overseas memberships, please write or email for current details.
The BFS reserves the right to raise membership fees.
Should the fee change, applicants for membership will be advised.

Email: syrinx.2112@btinternet.com